Surprise Me:
Brie's Submission

By
Red Phoenix

Surprise Me: Brie's Submission

Edited by Amy Parker, Proofed by Becki Wyer & Marilyn Cooper
Cover by CopperLynn
Phoenix symbol by Nicole Delfs

Adult Reading Material (18+)

Dedication

Of course I have to give love and kisses to MrRed,
He's my man!

I would also like to thank my cover designer,
Copperlynn. She is a long-time friend/fan and has
believed in Brie since the very beginning. She's never
stopped trying to find new ways to share Brie with
the world.

To all my wonderful fans who touch my life and make
me stronger!

CONTENTS

Fun with the Neighbors

S ince Brie had no idea what Master Anderson planned for the day, she'd dressed casually but with a stylish flair. She was still applying her makeup when she heard his call.

"Come out here, young Brie."

She hurried out of her room and found him in the kitchen, cooking breakfast. He looked up and smiled charmingly at her. "Sleep well?"

Brie frowned momentarily, thinking back on her dream. "I woke up from a bad dream this morning, but overall I had a restful sleep."

He directed her to a stool at the counter so she could watch while he cooked. His hands moved with grace and speed as he cut vegetables and added them to the omelet. At least Master Anderson understood and appreciated the beauty of a good omelet.

He moved around his kitchen with the skill and precision he brought to a session with the bullwhip. Brie would have bet that if she blindfolded him, he would have no problem navigating the kitchen as he cooked.

In no time, he slid a perfectly cooked omelet onto a plate and placed it in front of her. He handed Brie a fork, telling her, "Please eat while it's still hot."

She cut into his omelet of perfection and brought it to her lips, blowing lightly before taking a bite. Brie sighed in contentment. It was impossibly fluffy and light, a texture she'd never been able to achieve herself. "Wow, Master Anderson. Just, wow…"

He assembled his own omelet with finesse and sat next to her. "I like to start the day with eggs. Nature's perfect protein."

"Amen to that," she said, clinking forks with him. "I sure wish Sir liked eggs."

"It certainly makes you two an unfortunate pairing, doesn't it?"

She giggled. "Only if eating is important to him." She was about to take another bite when Master Anderson swept the plate from her. "Sorry, young Brie. I just noticed Ms. Courtney is out in her backyard."

"So?" Brie pouted, watching forlornly as he dumped their omelets in the trash.

"They won't be worth saving once they get cold," he assured her.

How Master Anderson could throw away a masterpiece like that was unfathomable to Brie, but the gleam in his eye had her more than a little curious—his mischievous nature was charming.

He explained to her, "I've wanted to teach my neighbor a lesson ever since I caught her snooping around my place uninvited. I insist on you joining me in the back, right now."

She nodded and asked, "What do you need me to do?"

"Simply follow my instructions. You may improvise where you deem appropriate." He escorted her out into the backyard and she could hear the neighbor talking loudly to a friend. The two seemed awfully chatty so early in the morning.

Brie scanned Master Anderson's yard. It backed up to a steep, mountainous hill and was landscaped with a wide variety of bushes and young trees with unusual cacti artfully placed throughout. For a splash of color, he'd added several types of columbine.

His well-manicured backyard maintained a manly feel that seemed to complement the solitary pole planted in the center. Brie knew *exactly* what that pole was used for, and understood the necessity of the privacy fence that separated it from his neighbors.

"Your yard is gorgeous, Master Anderson! Every bit as impressive as your other house, although the land-scaping is different."

"Knowing your plants and the climate they thrive in is the key," he informed her. "The environment up here is completely different than in town. Most homeowners fail to appreciate that." He stroked the leaf of a flourish-ing bush nearby, looking every bit the proud papa.

Master Anderson walked back over to her and whis-pered, "I'm going to retrieve the necessary items. Do not stray from this spot."

He spoke loudly so the women on the other side of the fence could hear, "Let's finish breakfast before we begin." He disappeared into the house, leaving Brie to eavesdrop on the ladies conversing on the other side of the fence.

"I don't have a clue, Wendy. All I know is that he works odd hours and is drop-dead gorgeous—as well as single."

"It seems he already has a girlfriend, Courtney. How else do you explain that girl being here so early in the morning?"

Courtney tsked dismissively. "I've never seen her before. Probably his sister visiting or something."

"I can't believe I let you talk me into coming. I'm missing my Pilates class for this, and you know how I get whenever I miss Pilates."

"I'm telling you, once you see this guy you'll be on your knees kissing my feet."

Brie smirked to herself. It seemed his neighbor, Courtney, was determined to set Master Anderson up with the Pilates girl.

He came back out grinning as he held up a set of leather bindings and his tool bag. Brie had to remind herself to breathe. She hadn't counted on a session with him, especially with a vanilla audience listening nearby.

Master Anderson declared boisterously, "I forgot your name, so I'll just call you 'baby' to avoid confusion."

"My na—" Brie started.

"No, I really couldn't care less what it is."

Brie bit her lip, smiling at his devilish humor. What would those poor women think? Little did they suspect he was just getting started.

"Kneel and open that pretty little mouth."

Brie obediently sank to her knees with her mouth slightly open in a pleasing manner. She looked up innocently, enjoying her role.

He handed Brie the tool bag and commanded, "Unzip it slowly. I want to you admire what's inside." She did as he asked, knowing the sound could easily be mistaken for the unzipping of pants. "Do you like what you see, baby?" he asked huskily.

She smiled.

"Of course you do," he answered for her. "Now take it out. I want you to handle it properly before I use it on you."

Brie heard an audible gasp on the other side of the fence and had to bite her lip to keep back the laughter. She took the bullwhip out of the bag and touched its deceptively smooth, braided leather. For something so pleasant to the touch, it definitely had a wickedly painful side to it.

"I want you to kiss it."

Brie leaned over and pressed her lips against the fierce tool. Her heart skipped a beat, her body still remembering its bite.

"That's it, baby. Pucker those pink lips and kiss the length of that bad boy."

Brie left a trail of kisses down the handle of the bullwhip.

Master Anderson took it from her. "Take that thing off," he said, pointing to her top. "I want those tits to bounce when we do this."

A utensil clattered onto the patio concrete on the other side of the fence. There was no doubt they had a captive audience.

Brie unbuttoned her blouse, and was about to undo her bra but Master Anderson shook his head. She handed him her shirt, grateful not to be naked in case Courtney decided to peek over the fence.

He draped it across a patio chair, warning her, "I will not be gentle with you."

"I like it rough," Brie replied, wanting the women eavesdropping to know this was a consensual encounter, in case they were considering calling the police.

Pointing to the wooden pole, he commanded, "Stand and present yourself over there."

Brie's stomach fluttered as she willingly walked up to it, unsure if she was prepared to take the harsh onslaught of his whip so early in the morning.

"Hands up, baby," he said in a deceptively amiable voice. He bound her wrists in leather and secured them to a hook attached to the post. He swept her hair away so that her back was exposed to him. Brie's nipples hardened in anticipation of what was coming—fear seemed to have that effect on her.

"Spread those legs."

When she did, he growled sensually. "Wider…"

Brie couldn't imagine what the ladies were thinking. She heard the swish of the bullwhip cut through the air as Master Anderson warmed up, but he did not crack it. She closed her eyes, the anticipation of contact almost unraveling her.

"No tears this time."

She whimpered in answer.

There was an angry huff from the other side of the

fence. Brie stifled her giggle. If he wasn't careful, Master Anderson might have a riot on his hands.

"My strokes will come hard and fast. Are you ready?"

Brie hesitated for dramatic effect before saying timidly, "Yes."

It was as silent as the grave on the other side of the fence.

When the first lash contacted her back, Brie was surprised to find it challengingly pleasant—a strike that was light but hard enough to stimulate the skin. She let out a passionate moan when the second lash found its way home.

"You like it hard, don't you?"

Brie enjoyed egging the women on with the naughty banter and purred, "The harder the better." She trusted Master Anderson understood she was only kidding.

He rained down a series of lashes, precise in his placement, with exactly the same intensity as the first. Truly, this man *was* a master of the whip.

Brie's cries were of pure, sexual bliss.

"Quiet, you'll wake the neighbors," he warned cheekily.

"You make it hurt so good..." she panted.

"It's true I know how to handle my tool," he replied in a playfully arrogant voice. "Hell, I've been stroking young heifers with it since I was a boy."

There was an audible gasp on the other side of the fence.

"But I'm becoming bored with this. Let's try something new—something I know you're not going to like."

He untied Brie from the pole and handed over her

blouse. With her skin still tingling from the quick bullwhip session, she buttoned it up and waited for his next command.

"Move over to the fence and bend over with your ass in the air."

She walked over to the spot he'd indicated, just opposite of the two ladies, and did as he'd instructed.

As Master Anderson approached he explained, "This isn't about you. This is about what I want. Understand?"

"But—"

"Not another word."

He came up behind her and handed her a set of gardening gloves. Then he leaned over and grabbed her hands, guiding them to a spiky weed. "Grasp it with both hands and pull hard."

The needlelike thorns pressed through the glove material and pricked her sensitive palms. It was slightly uncomfortable, so she whimpered pathetically for the benefit of their audience.

"I don't care if it hurts, baby. Pull on it like you mean it."

Master Anderson aided her by gripping the offending weed below her hands. With his help, the stubborn plant came up without any problem.

"That wasn't so bad, now was it?"

"Yes, it was," she complained with a grin.

"I want you to do it again."

She whined pitifully, "But it hurt…"

"I don't care if it hurt. Bend over and yank harder this time."

"That's it!" Courtney roared from the other side of

the fence, "For God's sake, leave that poor girl alone!"

Both women peeked over the fence in unison. If looks could kill, Master Anderson would have been struck dead on the spot.

He looked up at them innocently. "Howdy, ladies— sorry if we disturbed you. My girl here is wimpy when it comes to yard work."

Brie smiled up at them, her hands still clutching the plant.

The two women couldn't comprehend what they were seeing versus what they'd just heard. They stared at Brie, too flabbergasted to speak.

"I really hate weeding," Brie confessed with a shrug.

Courtney sputtered, "I…uh…we…uh…"

"We heard you doing things to this girl," Wendy insisted, looking accusingly at Master Anderson.

"Heard what, exactly?" he questioned, ignoring Wendy as he stared hard at his neighbor.

Master Anderson's gaze unnerved Courtney and she answered sheepishly, "Nothing. Come on, Wendy." The two slunk back down on their side of the fence and hurried into the house.

Once her sliding glass door slammed shut, Master Anderson threw back his head and gave a full-bellied laugh. When he was done he wiped away a pretend tear. "They make it too easy for me."

"Your devilish humor is going to get you in trouble someday, Master Anderson," Brie warned.

He pinched her cheeks, wiggling them gently from side to side. "You were brilliant, my little accomplice. That last little, 'But it hurt…' was the absolute kicker.

How could they resist a peek, in the name of all that is holy?"

As she walked back into the house, she stated casually, "You know, Courtney was just trying to pair you off with her friend."

Master Anderson smirked, looking back at his neighbor's house. "Really?"

"I thought you'd enjoy knowing that little tidbit. To think that your evil ways have caused you to miss out on the future Mrs. Anderson. Such a shame."

He ruffled her hair. "Totally worth it. The look on their faces when they peeked over to find you weeding—priceless!"

Mysterious Autumn

Lea honked her horn three times to let Brie know she'd arrived to pick her up. Brie was actually nervous about meeting Lea's new friend. All the mystery surrounding the girl, along with her unwillingness to meet on that first night, made Brie uneasy. Despite Lea's assurances that she would adore the girl, Brie still had serious doubts.

She apologized to Sir, who was on the phone, having taken a moment out of his busy schedule to check on her. "I'm sorry, Sir, but Lea's here."

"Not a problem, Brie. I'm glad you're finally getting to spend time with her."

Brie smiled into the phone. "But I hate to say good-bye to you."

"We'll see each other soon enough. Go enjoy your time with Lea."

"I love you, Sir."

"I love you too, babygirl."

She pressed the end button and stuffed her phone in her purse, skipping out the door to meet her best friend.

"Lea!"

Lea jumped out of her car and ran to the passenger side to give Brie a hug. "I'm going to squeeze you as much as I can while you're here. I've missed my Stinky Cheese."

The two hugged several times before hopping into Lea's beat-up excuse of a ride. The poor car was so full of dents it reminded Brie of a golf ball.

Once they were on the road, Brie asked her, "So, girl, where are we headed this fine Colorado evening?"

"We're going to do something a little daring to-night."

"Oh no. Now you have me worried."

Lea laughed, patting her knee. "You're going to love it. Trust me."

After the Kinky Goat incident, Brie wasn't taking any chances. "Out with it, Lea. Where are we headed?"

"To a skating rink, silly."

"What, like roller-skating?"

"Oh heck, no, that's for children. We're going ice-skating."

"But I can't ice-skate."

"Neither can I," Lea stated enthusiastically.

"If neither of us can skate, why the heck are we go-ing?"

"Don't be such a stick-in-the-mud, Brie. This is Autumn's favorite place."

Brie looked out the car window and grumbled, "My ass is going to be bruised by the end of the night."

"Then it's no different from a night at The Haven, now, is it?"

Brie turned to her and giggled. "I suppose you're right. So tell me, is this girl some kind of Olympic athlete or something? Is that the reason for all the secrecy?"

"Nah, Autumn is just like us." Lea bumped shoulders with Brie and in the process almost ran her car off the road.

Brie clutched the door handle and squealed, "Sir will kill you if we die tonight."

"How?" Lea joked. "Is he going to come up to Heaven and kill me just to prove a point?"

Brie burst out laughing. Dang, it was great being with Lea again. "I've missed you, woman! Sure wish you'd come back to LA."

"I miss you too, but I like it here. Like, seriously."

"Why? What does Denver have that LA doesn't?"

"The snowcapped mountains and changing seasons. I can't explain it, but I love it here. It's like the best of all worlds."

"Well, I know one thing this city doesn't have."

"What?"

"Me."

"Aww…Brie." Lea tried to give her a hug and almost ran them off the road again.

"Hands on the wheel, woman!"

Lea's infectious laughter filled the tiny car. "I promise no more hugs until we've made it safely to the rink. I don't need Sir going after my ghostly ass."

Brie giggled. "God, you're such a nut."

"And that's why you love me."

"Yeah, and the only reason I put up with all your lame-ass jokes."

"By the way, I've got another one for you."

Brie covered her ears. "Nope."

Lea pouted, her bottom lip quivering as she looked at Brie. Lea knew she couldn't resist that look.

"Fine," she sighed, "insult my sense of humor."

"Goodie! You know you're a kinky mom when…" Lea paused, waiting to make sure Brie was listening.

"When what?" Brie asked dryly.

"Your son's Boy Scout troop thinks you're the bomb because you helped them earn their merit badge for tying knots."

Brie chuckled despite herself. "That's barely funny."

She pointed to Brie's lips. "I heard you laugh. You know you love it."

"Well, only slightly…I think."

Lea grinned. "Oh, you'll be remembering that little joke and thinking of me when you're surrounded by your brood. Just you wait."

The idea of holding a tiny Sir in her arms made Brie's heart flutter. She couldn't really imagine it, yet the thought of having his child enchanted her.

Lea glanced over at her. "Hey, what's that adorable look on your face all about?"

Brie blushed. "It's nothing. Just glad to be with you again, girlfriend."

Once they'd pulled up to the ice-skating rink and parked, Lea got out her phone to text the girl they were meeting.

Lea smiled when she read the response. "Autumn is already here and can't wait to meet you."

"Great," Brie said, with more enthusiasm than she felt. Making a fool of herself on the ice was not her idea of fun, and she still had reservations about Lea's new friend.

Lea grabbed Brie by the arm and squeezed her tight. "I can't believe it. I have my bestest friend meeting my new best friend. I feel so lucky!"

Autumn was waiting for them in the main lobby, hiding in the shadows in the corner. Lea released Brie and went straight for her, pulling her away from the wall.

Brie noticed two things right away. First, the girl wore a scarf that covered most of her face. Second, she moved stiffly when Lea pulled her away from the wall. Neither was off-putting, just odd. Brie held out her hand and smiled at Autumn. "Hello. I've heard a lot about you from Lea. Well, that's not true. I've heard very little about you, just that Lea thinks you're the best thing to happen since sliced bread."

The girl's eyes twinkled as she took the hand Brie offered. "I've heard all about you, Brie. Lea can't stop talking about her favorite Stinky Cheese."

Brie gave Lea a sideways glance. "Stinky Cheese? Really, Lea? The two of us haven't even met yet and she's already calling me Stinky Cheese."

Lea shrugged, grinning like the Cheshire Cat but Autumn took pity on Brie.

"You're right, I haven't introduced myself properly. It's unfair that I know so much about you but you know nothing of me." She moved away from the main entrance and into a darkened hallway. With a graceful movement, Autumn unwound the scarf around her head and revealed her face to Brie. She had a deep scar running from her ear to her lip, underneath her right cheekbone. Autumn smiled hesitantly at Brie.

"There's no reason to cover your face. You're beautiful," Brie assured her.

"You're very kind to say that." She caressed the scar self-consciously. "I prefer to get to know people before I show my face. Normally I wouldn't be so bold with someone I've just met but, based on everything Lea's shared, I feel as if I know you already. Plus I have this good feeling about you—it's as if we've been friends for a long time."

Brie was honored Autumn felt that way. "I'm not sure if it's because Lea loves you so much or you're just naturally awesome, but I feel the same way."

Autumn's smile was genuine and warm. It made the scar on her face invisible to Brie.

Lea giggled, hugging both girls at the same time. "Now that you two have met, my life is complete."

Brie rolled her eyes.

"Lea is a bit over-the-top, but I like that about her," Autumn said, glancing at Lea with affection.

"I like that about Lea the Lame too," Brie agreed, pinching Lea's cheeks as if she were a child.

"So would you two like to skate now?" Autumn asked, gesturing to the rink on the other side of the large double doors.

Brie grimaced. "Sorry, but I don't know how to skate."

"I'd be happy to teach you both," Autumn offered.

Lea and Brie looked at each other and shrugged, giggling as they made their way to the skate rental counter while Autumn headed into the rink. "Meet you on the ice," she called to them.

"Sure thing," Lea answered, waving to her. "Hey, Autumn, what did the doctor say to the girl who fell on her bum while ice-skating?"

"I don't know," Autumn shot back enthusiastically.

"Do you want some ice for that?"

Autumn's twittering laughter echoed down the hallway.

"I seriously can't believe she laughed at that," Brie teased.

"I'll have you know that Autumn laughs at all my jokes."

"I'll try not to hold that against her."

Once they had their skates in hand, the girls walked through the double doors into the rink area. There Brie saw Autumn in all her glory. She'd shed her heavy clothes and wore only a simple top and white skirt. Brie watched in amazement as the girl floated on the ice, turning in graceful circles on two legs, one of which happened to be made of metal.

"She's incredible," Brie whispered to Lea.

"She really is," Lea agreed, "in so many ways." She hugged Brie again. "I just *knew* you two would hit it off!"

Autumn spent the evening patiently instructing them on the fundamentals of skating. She also had a few lame jokes of her own to add as they practiced skating around the rink.

"How do you know you aren't making the Olympic skating team?"

Lea almost tripped when she looked up from her skates to ask, "I don't know, Autumn—how do I know I'm not making the Olympic team?"

"Your coach keeps screaming, 'Let go of the railing! Let go of the railing!'"

When Lea started laughing, she promptly fell on the ice.

Brie quickly grabbed onto the railing to prevent the same thing from happening to her. "Hey, is that supposed to be a commentary on our skating abilities?"

Autumn skated past them going backwards, holding up both thumbs. "You're doing *grrreat*!"

Brie looked over and saw Lea struggling to get up off the ice. "Lea, I think your friend is toying with us."

After several failed attempts to get back on her feet, Lea gave up and crawled to the wall. "I'm afraid you're right, Brie. I think it's time for some hot cocoa."

"I'm right behind ya, sister."

"But ladies, I have so much more to teach you," Autumn called from the ice, doing a beautiful spiral before them.

"Another day, Autumn. I don't want you to abuse Brie too much on her first day meeting you."

"Wimps!"

"A wimp and proud of it," Brie shot back, holding up both thumbs.

Once they'd settled in a booth with hot chocolate in hand, Brie decided to ask the obvious. "So, Autumn, do you mind me asking what happened?"

"No, not at all. I was in a car accident when I was a kid. After I lost my leg, my mom decided to sign me up for ice-skating to give me something to focus on and strive towards." Autumn looked back longingly at the rink. "It's only on the ice I'm as graceful and beautiful as I feel in my heart."

Brie was touched by her words. "You're a strong person."

The girl picked up her Styrofoam cup and smiled at Brie. "I'm lucky to be alive, and I keep that to the forefront of my mind any day I start feeling sorry for myself."

"Those are words we all should live by," Brie replied, admiring her even more.

Lea gave Autumn a hug. "I told you she was something special."

"You know what I like about you, Brie?" Autumn asked, still nestled against Lea's big boobs.

Brie felt heat rise to her cheeks. "I can't imagine."

"You're a famous director, and you didn't bring it up all evening. You were just genuine and fun."

"I'm not famous, Autumn. Lea's been exaggerating."

Autumn sat back up and smiled at her. "I know who you are, Brie Bennett. I've been following your story ever since the documentary came out. It's the reason I was brave enough to approach Lea. She was such a goof on screen; I just *had* to meet her in real life."

"Aww…" Lea pressed Autumn's face back against her chest one more time. "I can't believe I'm goofy enough for you, friend."

"You're even goofier than me, and I didn't think that

was possible."

Brie enjoyed watching their friendly teasing. "So, Autumn, are you into the lifestyle yourself?"

"Oh no, I could never…"

"Too kinky for you?"

"No, it's just that I don't think I could handle being intimate with someone like that. I…I don't have the confidence. Besides, I'm much happier on the ice."

"Even though I've just met you, I can tell you're a beautiful person—and it's not just on the ice."

Autumn blushed a deep shade of crimson, then made a classic Lea move. "Why shouldn't you tell jokes while ice skating?"

Brie shook her head, knowing it was going to be bad. "No clue."

"Because the ice might crack up."

Lea and Brie started snickering, then broke out in giggles that wouldn't stop.

Autumn shook her head in amusement. "It wasn't that funny, but thanks."

The girls had another round of hot cocoa before heading home. Before they parted, Brie asked Autumn, "Do you mind if I give you a hug?"

"With kindred spirits, hugs are always welcome."

Brie wrapped her arms around the extraordinary woman. A sense of peace and wellbeing radiated from Autumn, surrounding Brie as she held her. "It was truly an honor to meet you tonight. Thanks for giving me a chance."

"Hey, I appreciate you putting up with me and my odd ways," Autumn said.

Brie turned to Lea. "And thank *you* for bringing us together, girlfriend."

"Actually, Brie, it was you and your film."

Brie paused to think about it. "I guess you're right. Amazing to think that everything we do has a ripple effect we're not aware of." She smiled at Lea and Autumn. "If you take it a step further, the three of us would never have met if Sir hadn't left his business card at the tobacco shop."

Brie smiled to herself. *Thank you, Sir!*

A Session with Clark

B rie was anxious about filming Ms. Clark again, and placed Tono's white orchid in her hair with trembling hands. *Help me to breathe, Tono,* she silently prayed.

She hadn't gotten a chance to talk privately with the Domme since Master Anderson's prank. Despite Lea's assurances, Brie was worried she might end up in the stockades during the session today. However, it was a risk worth taking since her producer, Mr. Holloway, had specifically requested she include a scene that featured the Dominatrix. The documentary was extremely important to Brie, and she was willing to do whatever was required to ensure Ms. Clark was part of it.

Brie took solace in the fact that the trainer herself had scheduled the session. Just like the first time, Ms. Clark surprised Brie with her willingness to help with the documentary, despite their many differences. She was unsure if it was because of the Domme's close relationship with Sir, or if there were other things in play she was unaware of. Regardless, Brie was determined to capture the beauty and allure of a skilled Domme on film. She owed the public no less.

Unfortunately for Brie, she arrived ten minutes late to the session through no fault of her own. Brie prided herself on being on time and fully expected to be reprimanded by the Domme, but Ms. Clark was the epitome of calm. She looked up when Brie entered the room.

"Good afternoon, Miss Bennett."

Her serene demeanor was startling, but it was not the only thing that struck Brie. The Domme had dressed in a sexy red corset and black hose, with dangerous-looking heels that ended in gold-tipped spikes. Her long blonde hair framed her flawless makeup, and her perfect lips sported the same vibrant red as the corset.

Ms. Clark was absolutely stunning, making it difficult for Brie to keep her eyes from straying back to the Domme as she set up her equipment.

"So, Miss Bennett, collared life treating you well?" Ms. Clark asked, a smile playing on her sensuous lips.

Brie stopped adjusting the camera to answer her. "Very well, Ms. Clark. I have grown tenfold under Sir's guidance."

"He seems to agree, and only has good things to say about you."

Brie cocked her head in surprise. "He talks about me to you?"

"Yes. We still keep in contact. Are you surprised by that?"

"I knew he called you on occasion, but I never suspected I was part of the conversation." Brie went back to work, hiding her smile.

Ms. Clark sighed in irritation. "I'm still not pleased you know as much as you do about my past, but I suppose it can't be helped. You are, after all, Sir's submissive. It's his choice what to share and to not share with you."

The way she said it put Brie on edge. Her words were true enough, but her tone of voice hinted that there were things Sir was *not* sharing with Brie. It upset her, but she refused to let her emotions muddy this opportunity to film the trainer.

"Ms. Clark, how will this scene play out today?"

"You will call me Mistress Clark during this session."

Brie nodded. "It will be my pleasure."

"I thought your audience would be interested in watching a Domme work with both a male and a female."

Brie's eyes lit up at the suggestion. She'd never seen Ms. Clark work with a man before, and she knew Mr. Holloway would approve. "If that's the case, where exactly in the room will both scenes take place? I want to make sure we have proper lighting."

Ms. Clark stood and walked slowly to the center of the room, turning around to face her. The Domme gestured to either side of her and gave Brie a beguiling smile.

It was unsettling—the allure of the woman was undeniable, and Brie found herself responding to it much the same as she would a confident Dom. She answered with a disinterested voice, not wanting her old trainer to pick up on her body's confusing reaction. "Perfect—that will make it easy for me."

Brie concentrated on the lighting while Ms. Clark set up her table of instruments. She glanced across the room and saw that the Domme had laid out a variety of canes of various lengths and widths, as well as a set of floggers. Brie remembered that the Dominatrix favored the cane, but she had never seen the woman wield it. She actually felt sorry for Lea.

When two unknown subs entered the room, Brie was taken aback. She'd naturally assumed that the Domme would be working with Lea for this scene.

The female submissive was stout, with a beautiful face, bleached hair and a boyish haircut, while the male was tall and lean with unusually long, brown hair. The two complemented each other well.

Brie watched them bow before Ms. Clark. They did not move or speak after bowing before their Mistress, and she did not acknowledge them as she finished setting up the table. Once she was done, she looked at Brie. "Ready?"

"Yes, Mistress Clark. I will simply film. I won't disturb the scene but, if at any point you wish me to stop, just signal to me."

"Good," she replied dismissively. Ms. Clark turned and addressed her subs. "Stand, Breeze and Leo. Thank Miss Bennett for the privilege of being filmed today."

They both stood gracefully and turned to Brie, bowing their heads slightly. "Thank you, Miss Bennett," they said in unison.

"My pleasure," Brie answered, smiling encouragingly at them. "There is no reason to be nervous about the camera or me. This is just a scene with your Mistress.

Don't even think about it."

Ms. Clark walked around her submissives, tracing her long fingernail over their chests. Both were wearing black, Leo in form-fitting boxers and Breeze in a sports bra and thong. "My subs know to focus their attention only on me. Anything less would require swift and painful punishment."

Brie shivered, having experienced Ms. Clark's punishment in the past—she never thought of a paddle in the same way after that session.

Ms. Clark smiled alluringly at Brie. "Are you ready to begin, Miss Bennett?"

"Absolutely, Mistress Clark—just say the word."

The Domme instructed her subs where to stand. The two stood in exactly the same position, with their hands held at their sides in an open and pleasing manner, legs spread comfortably apart, heads lowered in a submissive stance. Their pose alone was artfully sensuous, inviting play.

"We begin," the Domme announced, picking up a thin rattan cane from the table and slapping it against her hand as she walked around her subs, openly admiring the two. "Leo, handsome and compliant. And then there's Breeze, striking and willful."

She caressed Leo's leg muscles with her cane, and Brie could see his physical arousal caused by the simple contact. Ms. Clark whacked him playfully on the ass as she passed, and he grunted in satisfaction.

When she came up to Breeze, she put the cane between her legs and tapped from side to side. The girl opened her legs into a wider stance.

"Better."

Ms. Clark moved around to face the sub and used the side of the thin cane to stroke the girl's breasts. She then caressed the sub's thighs with the instrument, using a gentle touch like that of a lover.

The Domme stepped back and lightly bounced the instrument up the front of the sub's thighs. Ms. Clark skipped over her mound and continued to tap up her stomach, stopping just below the crease of her breasts.

The Mistress then moved behind the sub and started to travel leisurely up her legs with the cane, tapping over the roundness of her ass and up the back. The strength of the contact was still playful.

"Watch as I play with my sub," the Domme commanded Leo. He dutifully lifted his head and turned to watch the seductress at work.

Ms. Clark rubbed the girl's ass with the side of the cane in lazy circles, letting the sub know which area would be first to feel its sting. Brie held her breath, waiting for the moment.

With lightning-quick speed, the Domme cracked the cane three times on Breeze's ass. The girl moaned in pleasure, obviously liking the sting the cane delivered. Ms. Clark came up behind her, almost but not quite touching. "Head up, Breeze." The sub stared at the ceiling as the Domme wrapped her arm around her, rubbing the cane over the front of her thighs just below her mound. The next area had been selected…

Brie watched expectantly as the Mistress delivered three quick strokes to the girl's groin. The sub moaned again.

Ms. Clark looked into the camera as she spoke. "I know what you want, Breeze."

Brie's breath caught. The way Ms. Clark pronounced the name…she could have sworn the trainer was speaking directly to her. Brie bit her lip to stop any unintended expression, knowing the Domme was staring at her.

"But I'm not going to give it to you," the Domme announced, breaking contact with the camera and whispering to her sub loud enough to be heard, "Yet."

Ms. Clark tapped the end of the cane on each nipple before moving over to the male sub and roughly grabbing his chin, planting a firm kiss on his lips. She ran her fingernails over his chest with one hand, still holding the cane with the other. The way she held it was like a promise—and a warning.

"Breeze, you may watch."

The girl lowered her gaze from the ceiling and turned to observe. Brie appreciated the sexual charm of being paired with another sub. She'd experienced it once with Lea. Seeing and hearing another person being played with was a total turn-on, especially when you knew you would be next.

"Do not move, sub," Ms. Clark said as she rubbed his torso with her cane before sliding it down over his groin. She struck the cane against his cock three times, causing it to swell underneath the fabric. The Domme looked down and smiled. "Yes, you enjoy the feel of the cane, don't you?"

"I do, Mistress," he agreed.

"But you like it harder," she purred, moving over to the table to pick up a thicker cane made of bamboo.

"Hands behind your neck," she ordered.

He lifted his arms, showing off his chest and the large bulge in his boxers to the camera as Ms. Clark took her position beside him. It was a powerful scene, the virile male sub waiting to receive a caning from his stunning Mistress.

"Count out loud, Leo."

"Yes, Mistress."

Brie heard the satisfying thud as the bamboo made contact. Ms. Clark held it there for several seconds. Brie knew from experience that it allowed the sensation of the strike to dissipate throughout the body.

"One," Leo called out.

The Domme struck him again, harder the second time, and pressed the cane against his skin afterwards.

"Two," he said in a low, satisfied tone.

Each successive hit was slightly more intense than the last—she delivered them with impressive strength. The sub's shaft plainly showed what he thought of his Mistress' caning skills. She stopped at ten and rubbed the area with her palm as she kissed him deeply.

It was erotic and intimate.

She whispered something to Leo before breaking away and smiling at her other sub. "I have not forgotten you…"

Ms. Clark went back to the table and selected a cane braided in red leather. It was not as thin as the first, but similar in size. "Your Mistress knows your heart's desire, Breeze." She told the girl to hold out both hands.

The sub held them in front of her, palm side up.

"Good girl." The sensual way Ms. Clark said those

simple words caused goose bumps to rise on Brie's skin. The Domme placed the cane in the sub's grasp, then began to run her hands over the girl's body, not aggressively or crudely. They were light, romantic caresses that traveled near the sensitive areas but never quite touched.

The amorous look on Breeze's face showed through the camera lens. Ms. Clark not only had her two subs captivated, but Brie knew her audience would be as well. This filming session was pure gold, she could feel it in her bones.

The Domme took the cane from the girl and commanded, "Bend over and grab your ankles."

The sub put her hands on her knees and slowly slid them down to her ankles in a sensual move. Mistress and sub were an erotic pair, bewitching the camera with every movement.

"Would you like to wear my marks, Breeze?"

"I would be honored, Mistress."

"Hold the position and make no sound."

Ms. Clark moved beside her and held the cane away from the girl's fleshy ass, making her wait—making everyone wait—for the Domme's pleasure.

Brilliant! Brie mused.

The strokes came in quick succession, one after the other down her ass to her thighs. When Ms. Clark finally stopped, Brie let out a breath. The girl had not made a peep.

Ms. Clark knelt down and lifted the sub's head. "Again?"

"Yes, if it pleases you, Mistress."

The Domme stood and glanced briefly at the camera

with a confident look before she returned to her position. Again she made the sub wait to receive her attention. It was like riding a roller coaster and hanging at the top for those few seconds before falling.

The rain of rapping was as quick and thorough as the first set. The sub let out a moan at the end.

"I said no sound."

"Yes, Mistress."

Ms. Clark struck her swiftly, just a single stroke that had to hurt. The girl squirmed from the impact but remained silent. Another stroke landed seconds later.

"Stand. You took your punishment well, Breeze," the Domme complimented. The sub rolled gracefully up from her stance, a look of joy on her face despite the tears in her eyes.

Ms. Clark ran her hand over the girl's ass with a look of pride. "The marks look lovely on you, by the way. I knew they would."

"I love wearing your marks, Mistress," Breeze answered breathlessly.

Ms. Clark hovered achingly near the girl's mouth for a few seconds before kissing her. She broke the passionate kiss to put the cane down on the table, instructing the sub to join Leo.

Breeze moved beside Leo, the sides of their feet touching so they were connected physically as they stood before their Mistress.

Ms. Clark returned to the male sub, tracing her fingers over his jawbone. Brie could see a subtle shiver ripple through his body at her touch. He was on fire for her.

"I will end today's session with you together."

"Thank you, Mistress," he said gruffly.

She went back to the table and picked up the two floggers. "Relax and enjoy your reward."

The Domme started out caressing her subs by running the multiple tails of the floggers lightly over their skin at the same time. It was gentle and tender, a moment of connection between the three of them before she began.

Ms. Clark stepped away and began to swing the floggers in the air. She swung in large, lazy circles that landed on their skin with light thuds. Both submissives were smiling. Brie knew the pleasant feel of the flogger and felt a twinge of jealousy as she watched.

Soon the Domme switched the pattern, doing simultaneous figure eights. It took skill to deliver both strokes with equal strength while keeping a consistent rhythm between the two floggers. The pleasant sound of leather against skin filled the room as Ms. Clark increased the power of her strokes.

The visual effect of the dual floggers flying in the air was stunning to watch, but the graceful movement of the Domme wielding the tools was even more impressive. Brie could not take her eyes off her.

Ms. Clark changed things up again by swinging in tight circles while increasing the speed, so that the contact made was quick and intense. She moved her attention down to their asses, causing a rippling effect on their fleshy buttocks as the floggers made contact. It was sensual to watch, and hearing both subs groan with pleasure made it that much hotter.

Brie shifted in her chair, grateful she'd remembered to bring a towel this time. She knew Marquis Gray would have been proud of her forethought.

The Mistress ended her scene by slowing her swings and returning to figure eights. It was fascinating to watch the floggers hang in the air as they leisurely danced over the submissives' red skin.

Ms. Clark put the floggers down on the table and returned to her subs. She began to caress the backs of her submissives, whispering as she gently touched them. After several moments, she looked up at Brie and signaled her to stop filming.

While Brie was packing up her equipment, Ms. Clark walked over to her. "You and I should talk sometime, Miss Bennett. There are certain things we need to discuss."

"Yes, Ms. Clark." Brie wasn't sure what the Domme wanted to chat about but, before she ever set up a meeting with her old trainer, she would have to talk to Sir. "Thank you for today's session. It was truly exquisite to watch."

The Domme arched her eyebrow and asked, "You enjoyed yourself, did you? I'm curious, Miss Bennett, what appealed to you more? The play with the male sub or the play with the female?"

Certain it was a loaded question, Brie grabbed her last remaining items and hurriedly stuffed them into her bag. She decided to answer the question with a compliment. "You have delivered a beautiful example of both, Ms. Clark. It will be interesting to see how the public reacts. I don't think you could have done a better job representing both ends of the spectrum."

Unsure of Ms. Clark's motives, Brie rushed out of the room before the Domme could respond or ask a follow-up question.

Seeds of Doubt

Brie waited impatiently for Sir to call. He had yet to confirm a time or a date for his arrival in Denver and she was extremely unhappy about it. She *needed* to feel his strong arms around her, especially now, with all the nagging doubts swimming in her head.

Lea had casually mentioned the fundamental requirement of open communication between D/s partners, and the fact was that Brie had been hiding something from Sir for the last few days. Tonight she was not going to dishonor him or their relationship any longer by being a coward.

We're condors, she reminded herself when her phone finally rang.

"Good evening, Brie. I apologize for the lateness of the call."

"I don't mind, Sir. I'm just happy to hear your voice."

"How did filming go today?"

"Mistress Clark was amazing, Sir. Truly amazing! I'm still blown away by the scene and I've watched it five times."

"Mistress Clark? Why 'Mistress'?"

Brie giggled self-consciously. "She asked me to call her that while I was filming today. It slipped out just now." She immediately changed the subject, not willing to wait any longer and possibly lose her courage to confront him. "Any idea when you will be coming, Sir?"

"Actually, yes. I'll be boarding the plane tomorrow. Should be landing in Denver early Friday morning."

"Oh, I can't wait! I feel like it's been months, not days, since I've seen you."

"I agree, it does seem an unnaturally long time apart."

Before she lost her nerve, she asked, "Sir, this may seem silly, but I've been getting a weird vibe here and want to ask you something."

He chuckled. "A weird vibe, you say?"

She closed her eyes, forcing herself to say the thing she had been afraid to voice out loud to anyone. "Sir, are you keeping something important from me?"

The line was silent on the other end.

As the moments dragged on, Brie's fear increased.

"Sir?"

His next question did nothing to relieve her concerns. "Is there a reason you're asking, Brie?"

"There are several reasons, actually. First, Baron told me he was sorry to hear about your troubles with your mother, and this afternoon Ms. Clark seemed to imply that you're not being completely open with me. Then there was the dream I had the other night."

"A dream?" He laughed, but it sounded forced.

"I can't remember what happened, but I know your mother was part of it."

The dead silence on the other end was frightening to her.

"Sir, you *are* keeping something from me, aren't you?" When he didn't answer, she demanded, "I have a right to know! I remember when I had to kneel on rice because I kept something from you. What consequence is there if you do the same to me?"

"You don't know what's happened."

"Exactly! We're condors, Sir. Does that mean *nothing* to you? Why does everyone else seem to know, but the person closest to you is left in the dark?"

"Brie, I think it would be best if we both returned to LA, where we can discuss this in person, alone."

Her heart sank. The tone of his voice let her know it was far more serious than she'd imagined. When she hung up the phone, she felt completely numb. It wasn't until she had made it to the bed and was curled up in the blankets that she finally broke down and cried.

Unfamiliar Territory

B rie woke up from a dream that involved Tono and a trail of orchids. She stretched out her arms above her head with a huge smile on her lips, the gentle presence of the Asian Dom still lingering. That smile died as soon as she remembered her phone call with Sir.

Rather than revisit those unwelcome feelings, she got up from her bed and walked to the desk in the corner. She opened the drawer, thrilled that Master Anderson had stocked it with stationary.

She pulled out several sheets of paper and a well-sharpened pencil. Brie stared at the writing instrument for a moment. How long had it been since she'd written with a pencil?

Inventory at the tobacco shop…

With that thought, a flood of memories came to mind: Mr. Reynolds' fatherly smile, that lazy ass Jeff, all those damn cigarettes—and Sir.

Brie shook off the feeling of sadness that threatened to smother her and began her letter.

Dear Tono,

I woke up this morning thinking of you and decided I should write you a letter.

I can't tell you how much I disliked leaving Japan, but I'm grateful for the time I got to spend with you, and for the chance to know your father before his passing. I will never forget honoring his memory with your family at his wake. It is something I'll always hold dear.

I'm beginning to understand why you chose to stay behind. There are times we must do what is right, even though it's hard and might tear us up inside. I respect you for remaining true to your values, especially when it comes at great cost.

I hope, with all my heart, you are able to find a balance where you can fulfill your duty to your mother and still honor your own needs. I think back on that night of glowing rope, the erotic beat of the music and the talent of your hands, and I know you have hit on something revolutionary. I hope you pursue it further, maybe even find your escape in it when you have need.

My time in Denver has been crazy. Lea is as full of bad jokes as ever, and wants me to share one with you. If you would like me to subject you to the torture, just say the word and I will include it in my next correspondence. Lea also introduced me to a new friend she met because of my documentary.

Autumn is truly amazing, Tono. Despite losing her leg as a child, she glides on the ice like an angel. I admire her strong spirit, and hope to hang out with her again soon. How cool that my film brought those two together. I just love that!

Although the training center in Denver is very different from the one in LA (practical jokes are the norm here), it seems to have a positive effect on the staff. Even Ms. Clark seems happy.

I think you should know I wear the beautiful comb you gave me whenever I film now. I can't tell you the number of times I hear your reassuring voice reminding me to breathe... Thank you for the positive influence you are in my life.

Love, Brie

Writing to Tono Nosaka had a calming effect on her, as if she'd actually spent time in his presence. She sealed up the letter, saying aloud, "*Domo arigato*, Tono."

Brie spent her afternoon with Lea at a nearby park, under the colorful foliage of a stunning Colorado fall. They lay out on a large blanket, side by side, relaxing in the warmth of the autumn sun. The sky was a spectacular shade of blue, something Brie had never seen before.

"Is it extra blue because we're a mile above sea level?" she asked.

Lea shrugged, turning her head lazily towards Brie

and smiled. "I don't know and don't care. I just love being here." She looked back up at the sky and took in a deep breath.

Brie did the same, breathing in the unique scent of fall. It reminded her of pumpkins, trick-or-treating and dressing in silly costumes as a child in the midwest. She'd missed that smell in California, but hadn't realized it until now.

"I wish I could stop time and just lie here in the sun forever."

"And look like a mummified piece of burnt bacon after a few weeks? No, thank you!" Lea replied, elbowing her.

"You know what I mean," Brie scolded gently.

"Yes. You don't want to face Sir."

Brie sighed in misery, vexed her friend knew her so well. "No, I don't. It makes it that much worse that everyone knows what's happened except me."

A tear fell down her cheek.

"I feel like a big joke, Lea."

Her friend rolled onto her side to face Brie, propping her head up with her hand. "No, girlfriend. No one feels that way about you. None of us would have known anything if the press hadn't gotten wind of it, and what we know is only what we've heard on TV."

"Why didn't you say anything to me?"

"Because Master Anderson asked me not to when he realized you didn't know. Seeing as we're besties, he figured it would come up in conversation, and he felt strongly that Sir should be the one to tell you."

"Well, I'm asking you now."

Lea groaned and lay back down, looking up at the sky. "I can't."

"Why?" Brie cried. "You're my best friend."

Lea turned towards her again, fidgeting with a stray thread on the blanket. "I know, and it's killing me not to say anything, but it wouldn't be fair to Sir."

"It's not fair to *me*," Brie complained.

Lea looked around apprehensively, then leaned close and whispered, "Okay, I'll only tell you that it was all over the news a few days before you showed up. It has to do with his mother and it's not good."

"Is Ruth coming after Sir again?"

Lea shook her head sadly. "No, nothing like that."

"What, then?" Brie pleaded.

"Look, sweetie, there has to be a reason he didn't tell you when you were in Japan. You'll have to give him the benefit of the doubt until you talk to him in person."

Brie put her hands to her face, covering her eyes to keep from crying. "I remember when Baron spoke about her; I sat there like a complete idiot complaining about how crazy she was. I should have known something was up when he acted so strangely. Then there was Ms. Clark. She mentioned that Sir was keeping things from me just before we started to film." Brie rolled away from Lea, staring at the mountains in the far distance. "All of which makes me feel like a fool."

Lea scooted over and hugged her, pressing her large boobs against Brie's back. "No one thinks you're a fool. We're just worried about you two."

Brie curled up into a ball. "I don't want to go home, Lea. I'm so angry with Sir for putting me in this situation, but I'm terrified that whatever he's hiding will tear us apart."

Lea squeezed her tighter. "Nothing can tear you two apart."

"I thought that once, but I'm not so sure now…"

Lea rolled Brie back over and said forcibly, "Don't think like that, not even for a second."

The tears started, and Brie was defenseless to stop them.

Lea wiped them away, stating in a serious tone, "A condor pair were nibbling on a dead clown. The male condor asked the female, 'Does this taste funny to you?'"

"Oh, Lea," Brie groaned, but as she mulled it over in her head it struck her as perfect. The joke not only referred to their condor love but hinted at her cooking skills. She smiled, but complained as she did so. "I hate that I love your bad jokes."

"I know, honey."

Master Anderson saw Brie off at the airport early the next morning, wearing his cowboy hat and tight-fitting blue jeans. He tipped the brim of his black hat as he said goodbye at the entrance of the security line. "Tell Thane I expect you two to return. He owes me."

Brie tried to sound more positive than she felt. "Sure."

Master Anderson lifted her chin, his intense green eyes boring into hers. "Young Brie, Thane is dedicated to you. Do not doubt that, even if current circumstances suggest otherwise."

She looked down at the floor, unable to look at him when she admitted, "It's humiliating to be the last to know."

"Look at me."

Brie looked up, facing his penetrating gaze.

"Are the opinions of others more important than his?"

She shook her head slowly.

"Instead of worrying what others think, what you should be concerned with is the fact that he felt the need to protect you. Knowing Thane, only something extreme would evoke such a reaction from him."

"And you know what it is, don't you?"

"Although I know what's happened with his mother, I don't know Thane's reaction to it. He hasn't spoken to anyone—and that distresses me."

Brie suddenly felt ashamed. The whole time she'd been fuming about being shut out, not once had she considered Sir's emotional state. Something dreadful must have happened for him to isolate himself like that.

She told Master Anderson with renewed conviction, "Sir has called me home to talk. I trust we can work through it, whatever it is we have to face."

"You'd better, young Brie, or I will lose all hope that true love exists."

She smiled. "It does, Mr. Anderson, and your turn is coming."

Brie squealed when he lifted her off the floor in his strong arms. "What? Are you convinced that if you keep saying that, it'll make it come true?"

She met his gaze under the brim of his cowboy hat. "I only speak the truth, Mr. Anderson."

He chuckled as he put her back down, spanking her lightly on the bottom as if she were a child. "Run along, young lady, and bring comfort to your man."

She scooted towards the line but looked back at him, struck by how handsome he looked. "Thank you for this week…and for the candid talk."

He tipped his hat to her. "Anytime, little heifer."

She giggled, finding it humorous that he'd just called her a cow—and she liked it. "Be off with you, Mr. Cowboy. Go find yourself a new heifer to play with."

He nodded towards two girls at a magazine rack nearby, who'd been staring at him. "Actually, I've just spied my next conquest."

Brie waved one last time as she settled into line, smiling to herself as she watched him heading towards the girls. Her smile faded when he walked past the two and headed out the doors. She sighed with frustration but sent out a thought to him. *Don't lose hope, Master Anderson. Your day is coming.*

She got on the plane feeling more hopeful than she had before, because of her talk with Master Anderson. She truly believed that condor love was an impenetrable force, but she'd forgotten that in her shock. Unfortunately, when she landed in LA, Sir's text message rekindled her doubt.

I will meet you at home.

Brie frowned, disappointed that he would not be picking her up at the airport, but she took solace in the word 'home'. It spoke of warmth and comfort—a safe place to gather in the storm.

She felt a mixture of excitement and dread as she entered their apartment. Although she longed to see Sir again, she did not want to face the confrontation about to take place. Brie was disappointed to find the apartment dark and silent as she walked in.

She set her luggage down in the hallway, noting that the smell of Sir lingered in the air, which hinted to the fact that he'd been there recently. She glanced around their place and was startled to see her journal haphazardly thrown on the coffee table, along with other items from his recent trip. She walked over to her beloved journal and picked up the wrapped package. Sir had never even opened it.

What did that mean?

She walked into the bedroom and placed it in its normal resting place inside the drawer of her nightstand. Brie turned away, feeling profoundly hurt. A sense of foreboding gnawed at her heart, knowing that whatever Sir was hiding truly *did* have the potential to tear them apart.

What had Ruth done this time? How was the witch planning to ruin their lives now?

She decided to do the only thing that would bring her peace. After unpacking her suitcase, she lit a fragrant candle and turned out the lights. Then she slowly undressed and knelt at the front door, waiting for Sir.

Brie closed her eyes and commanded herself not to

dwell on the *what ifs*. Instead she thought back to the last time they'd been together, reliving it in her mind. The night before she'd left Japan—a precious memory of hers.

"Let me make love to you before we say goodbye," Sir told her, pushing her gently onto the bed. "Death has a way of helping you to appreciate what you have..."

She closed her eyes as he undressed her, desperate for the healing power of his touch.

"Right now all that exists is you, me and this moment in time." Her heart melted when he growled those words into her ear. She needed this cherished intimacy with Sir before she left his side, bound for Denver.

Things had been difficult with the passing of Tono's father—so many raw emotions exposed—but it was knowing that Tono Nosaka would not be returning to America that absolutely crushed her. It was tragic that the talented Dom would be staying in Japan to care for his ungrateful mother, giving up everything he loved and worked hard for.

Brie hadn't been able to shake off the feeling of grief until Sir had wrapped her in his loving embrace. "This is all I need," she confessed.

He kissed her tenderly. "I agree."

Brie mulled over those simple words, as she knelt waiting for him in the dark. They held more significance now that she understood. That night he'd kept his terrible secret inside as he made love to her, finding his escape in her embrace—and she had been oblivious. Instead of concentrating on his own pain, he had focused on relieving hers.

Time had seemed to stop when he began kissing her lightly, trailing a path from her neck down to her stomach, making a leisurely detour to kiss and suckle her breasts…

"You have gorgeous breasts, babygirl," Sir complimented as he kneaded and rolled them in his fingertips. He sucked and flicked his tongue against her erect nipples until her pussy ached with longing. Continuing lower, he licked and nibbled her stomach, causing her entire body to focus on his mouth as she anticipated his wicked attention to her clit.

That first, long, drawn-out lick made her shudder with desire. Sir tasting her wetness, seeming to savor it, made her feel sexually irresistible. She pressed her mound against his skilled tongue, begging for more of his attention.

Sir grabbed her ass cheeks and dived into her, lapping, sucking and teasing her pussy with his mouth. It was obvious that he took as much pleasure in eating her as she did in sucking him. She tilted her head back as she grasped his head, surrendering to his tongue.

"You will come many times tonight," he informed her. "Not because I command it, but because I plan to love your body well."

She moaned as the first orgasm began to build in intensity.

"Don't resist me tonight, babygirl. Let your body

respond freely."

She closed her eyes, overwhelmed by the love flowing from him. She let her climax build until it reached a
glorious level before letting go, needing him to feel how
much he pleased her.

"That's my good girl…" he murmured between her
legs. Sir rode out her orgasm with his tongue pressed
against her pulsating clit, then he moved slowly down
her legs, teasing her with sensual nibbles and licks. He
stopped at her feet, tickling them with light kisses until
she giggled and squirmed.

Sir paused, looking at her intently, the smile on his
lips about doing her in. "Lie still and let me have my way
with you."

Brie willingly opened her legs to him again and
purred, "Have your way with me, Thane."

Using his given name had a definite effect on Sir. He
hesitated for a second before crawling between her legs.
He stopped to gaze down into her eyes before taking
her. "I count on your love more than you know."

At the time, she'd thought he'd meant it as a sweet
nothing, but now she understood he'd been speaking
from a heart overwhelmed with pain.

Brie was brought back to reality by that revelation.
She swallowed back tears, straightening her posture. One
sobering thought echoed in her mind as she knelt on the
floor waiting for him…

Sir needed me that night.

She'd been blind to his pain, greedily receiving the
love he offered, ravenous for its healing power. All the
tension and sadness caused by her week in Tokyo

dissolved the moment he'd entered her. Afterwards she'd lain in his arms, exhausted but content, reflecting on his earlier statement that death had the ability to help a person appreciate what they have.

Brie distinctly remembered looking at his handsome face as she caressed his strong jaw, and being filled with a deep sense of gratitude.

In response, he'd taken her hand and placed it over the brand on his chest.

The Truth

When she heard the jingle of keys as the door was unlocked, her heart almost stopped. This moment before confrontation was excruciatingly cruel; the knowledge that it could either end well or in complete disaster.

Think before you speak, but don't hold back, she commanded herself.

The door swung open, but Sir stayed in the hallway for a moment before entering their apartment. He shut the door and walked over to her, placing his hand on her head. A flood of energy passed between them, even though neither had spoken. When he removed his hand, she looked up at him expectantly.

"Stand, Brie."

The use of her given name was significant in this situation. Although he had accepted her submission by placing his hand on her head, Sir wanted to speak to her as an equal.

Brie stood up gracefully, keeping her head bowed, suddenly aware how naked she felt standing before him—it was a new and unwelcome feeling.

In a move uncharacteristic of Sir, he took off his jacket and covered her with it. Rather than it being a tender gesture meant as comfort, it made her feel cold inside. Something was fundamentally wrong between them.

"Would you like a drink?" he asked.

It was only ten in the morning, but she realized he must still be on Japan time. "No thank you, Sir."

He gestured that she should take a seat on the couch while he fixed himself a martini. She listened to the ice clinking in the metal shaker. Normally the sound of his vigorous shaking brought a thrill, but today it only caused her concern.

Sir needs a drink to talk to me...

When he came out of the kitchen, he avoided looking at her as he walked to the window and gazed at the city below. Sir took several sips of his drink before speaking.

"I know this was unfair to you."

Brie let out a sigh of relief. At least he'd acknowledged it. "I want to know what happened, Sir."

He shook his head, taking another sip. She sensed his emotional walls go up with that simple request. Was he going to keep it from her even now?

"I deserve to know."

He glanced at her briefly, then looked back over the city. "How much do you know already?"

Brie got up from the couch and walked over, unhappy with the distance between them—both physical and emotional.

"Almost nothing, because no one would talk to me about it. However, I'm certain it involves your mother, because I was told it made the national news."

"I didn't anticipate that. Why the hell would it make the news?" he muttered, tilting his glass back to finish the rest of its contents.

Brie pulled at the long sleeves of Sir's jacket to expose her hands, then she drew near to him, touching him lightly on the arm. He lowered his head, a look of torment clouding his eyes.

"Tell me…please," she whispered, standing on tiptoes to kiss him on the mouth.

His lips were unresponsive, but she saw tears in his eyes. "I'm a mess, Brie."

"Condors, Sir."

He stared at her for a moment before nodding. Sir put down his glass and led her to the kitchen. He pulled out a chair for her at the table, then went into the pantry, bringing out the bag of rice. He plopped it on the kitchen table, sitting down on the chair opposite her. "When I'm done, if you deem it necessary, I will kneel on rice."

A smile tugged at her lips. "Fine. I'll make that determination after you explain your silence to me."

He stared at Brie, the tortured look in his eyes breaking her heart, but no words came forth. She met his gaze and waited patiently.

Sir finally cleared his throat, stating, "I received news of my mother while we were in Tokyo."

Brie nodded encouragingly.

"I didn't see the point of burdening you with it at the

time."

"Bu—"

He shook his head. "You were already stretched emotionally trying to support Tono and truthfully...I could not process the news myself."

A chill ran down Brie's spine as she thought back on the trip. "I know exactly when you got the news. You were different in the car after I visited Tono's father."

Sir nodded. "I *did* receive the call at the hospital while you were talking to Master Nosaka." He looked at her suspiciously. "But how could you possibly know that?"

"You were different, Sir. I could sense it, but simply assumed that seeing Tono's father on the verge of dying had brought up bad memories for you."

He frowned. "I failed to realize how adept you are at reading people. It's a gift and a curse."

She took his hand in hers and squeezed it. "Not a curse, Sir. It's a characteristic condors share. Please tell me what's happened with your mother."

"You really don't know?" he asked in disbelief.

"No one would tell me, out of respect for you."

"I have good friends, I suppose," he said half-heartedly, staring past her.

"You do, Sir."

He let out a long sigh, putting his hands to his temples as he closed his eyes. "There was an earthquake in China."

"Oh, my God, is Ruth dead?"

Sir opened his eyes and shook his head slowly, his eyes clouded with pain. "My mother was providing relief in a remote area deep in the interior of China. She wasn't found for days after the quake. How ironic is that? She was there to provide medical relief, yet there was none to be had when she needed it."

He looked away, grimacing. "Doctors tell me if my mother had received immediate care, she would have survived the incident. Instead she lies in a coma, connected to feeding and breathing tubes to keep her alive."

Brie got up from her chair and moved over to him, settling on his lap when he offered it. She hugged him tightly, whispering, "I'm so sorry."

"How many times have I wished she would die? But damn it, not like this…" He pressed her against his chest. "This is my fault, Brie. I sent her there as penance, and now she is frozen between life and death."

Brie pulled away and looked him in the eye. "What's happened is not your fault. You gave her a second chance even though she didn't deserve it."

He growled fiercely. "As much as I hate the Beast, I never wanted this!"

Brie knew exactly what was needed. "We should go see her, Sir. Right now." She tried to get off his lap, but he held her tighter.

"That's where I just came from. As soon as you left, I flew to China to assess her condition and see if anything could be done."

"Oh…" Brie couldn't hide how much not being included hurt.

Sir lifted her chin, forcing her to look him in the eye. "Even though you are angry with me now, I do not regret keeping this from you. I was too full of rage and sorrow at the time." He gazed at her with tenderness. "Truthfully, Brie, I did it to protect you—from me."

"But I'm not afraid of you, Sir," she declared defiantly.

"You should be. Although I would never hurt you physically, I'm quite capable of tearing you apart."

"You should know that I can bear the brunt of your anger, as long as I understand its source."

He groaned as he released his hold on her. "When I shared that I have my demons, it was not simply idle talk, Brie. I *am* my mother's son. I know you admire my ability to assess people and deliver what they need, but what you don't understand is that it can also be used to harm them. There are times I have to fight against the urge to destroy."

She cradled his face in her hands. "You are a good man, Thane Davis. You would not harm me."

He sighed, shaking his head. "That day, when I got the news…it festered inside me like poison, growing in intensity with each passing second. If I had not retired into the bedroom, I guarantee you would have been hurt."

"It's not healthy to hide things from each other," Brie insisted.

"You were having a hard enough time dealing with Tono. Remember?"

"But I could have handled it, Sir. Being left in the dark is far, far worse."

"Don't you understand, Brie? I needed time to process and compartmentalize my feelings before they controlled my actions and I did something I would regret."

"While I believe you felt that you were protecting me, I'm still resentful you let me fly off to Denver like a clueless idiot, believing things were okay, while you faced your mother's situation alone."

He closed his eyes and nodded, taking in her words. "Yes, it was unfair to send you away unaware, but it brought me comfort to know you were happy and safe."

She pressed her forehead against his. "I love that you want to protect me, Sir, but I'm not fragile. I won't break."

He brushed her cheek tenderly. "You must allow me the space I need, Brie."

"I can't be the last to know. We're partners, Sir."

He huffed in frustration. "How could I know the media would cover it here in the States? I didn't intend to put you in that situation, and there is no way in hell I could have foreseen that."

"Fine," she conceded, "as long as it doesn't happen again."

He leaned forward, his mouth centimeters from her lips. "Rice or no rice?"

As tempting as those lips were, Brie avoided the kiss and reached for the bag. She looked at it thoughtfully before stating, "You deserve to be punished, regardless of your good intentions. However, I'm a reasonable submissive and won't punish you—this time. As long as it never happens again."

"Rest assured I shall come to you first, but I still need my space. Forcing the issue will only be met with resistance."

"I respect your need for space, but don't take too long to include me. It hurts."

He kissed her on the lips, murmuring, "Forgive me, Brie."

His tone was light, but she saw the tortured look in his eyes when he lifted her off him and picked up the bag of rice to return it to the pantry.

Sir hadn't spoken about his feelings after seeing his mother—he'd purposely avoided the issue—but Brie was willing to give him more time, grateful they had successfully navigated this first crisis.

She smiled when he came back to the table, saying as she sank to the kitchen floor, "Let my lips show you just how much you've been missed, Sir."

Coen's Lesson on Spanking

It didn't take long for Brie to realize they hadn't navigated anything at all. She could see Sir was struggling under the weight of his emotions, but he still was unwilling to speak of them. Instead, he became uncharacteristically moody and withdrawn as he devoted his time and focus to work in an attempt to escape the pain that threatened to consume him.

Brie felt his torment and longed to share the burden he was carrying. Since he was unwilling to confront it, she broached the subject one morning while sipping coffee.

"Sir, can we talk?"

He looked at her warily but answered, "Certainly, Brie."

She took his hand, hoping the contact would ease his building anxiety. "You haven't really told me how you feel about what's happened to your mother."

Brie could feel the walls instantly rise as he tried to pull away from her, but she'd been prepared for that. "I can see it's eating you up inside, Sir."

His nostrils flared. "Why bring up unpleasant emotions? Talking about it will only drag out memories of a past I have no interest in revisiting."

She smiled at him sympathetically. "But keeping those feelings buried is killing you. I see it in your eyes; I feel it in your touch."

His response was curt and dismissive. "I don't want to discuss it with you."

Brie squeezed his hand, maintaining their connection. "You told me to give you space and I've done as you've asked. However, things are not getting better. It's only getting worse."

"Brie," he snarled menacingly, "don't force me down this path with you. You will regret it." He stood up and broke away from her, grabbing his car keys. "I'll be out all day. Don't bother calling."

Brie swallowed the feelings of rejection as the door slammed shut. Every time she thought they were moving forward as a couple, she found herself in the same place, excluded and alone.

She understood that Sir had been reluctant to take her as his submissive for this very reason—she *knew* that—but it didn't make his rejection any easier.

Brie was scheduled to meet with Master Coen that day to film a scene for the new documentary. Although she was sorely tempted to cancel, she didn't want to disrespect the Headmaster's time.

God, how she wished Lea was around—hell, even Mary would have been a comfort to her right now.

Brie got up and dutifully went to the bathroom to apply her makeup, putting her hair in a ponytail to avoid having to style it. She added Tono's white orchid to give herself a more finished look. Out of respect for Master Coen, she dressed in a business suit and high heels, when all she really wanted was to slip on a pair of comfortable sweats.

Pulling into the parking lot of the Submissive Training Center brought back memories of more carefree days, when life had seemed full of promise and laughter. She got out of her car and walked to the entrance, smiling when a young man graciously opened the door for her. She thanked him—images of Faelan dancing in her head.

She hadn't thought of Todd Wallace in ages, and hoped Faelan and Mary were doing well together. No one had heard from the couple since they'd joined the commune. Cell phones were not allowed there, and Mary hadn't made any effort to contact Brie since she'd left.

You'd better be having the time of your life, bitch, Brie thought with a grin.

"Hello, Miss Bennett, would you like me to inform Headmaster Coen that you are here?" the receptionist asked pleasantly.

"Please."

Brie stood beside the welcome center, lowering her gaze to avoid eye contact when she noticed some of the male students approaching on their way to business classes. She'd been trained well, but she jumped like a newbie when the receptionist announced, "Good morning, Marquis Gray."

Brie held her breath, drumming up courage before turning around and greeting him with a bright smile.

"Miss Bennett, what brings you here?" the ghostlike Dom asked.

"I'm filming a scene with Headmaster Coen today."

"Ah, for the new documentary, I take it."

"Yes, I'm hoping to film a few scenes here for the second one."

He took the mail the receptionist handed him and looked it over before nodding to Brie. "I trust the filming will go well. Please see me after you're done."

Brie's smile faltered for a moment, but she responded appropriately, "It would be my pleasure, Marquis Gray."

The elevators opened and Master Coen walked out, as impressive-looking as the first time she'd met him—all muscle, but with a sophisticated air about him.

"You've returned, Miss Bennett."

"I can't seem to stay away, Headmaster Coen."

He chuckled good-naturedly as he guided her into the elevator. Master Coen led her to his office—Sir's old office. Again, memories assailed her as she glanced around the room. "Is this year's class performing well?" she asked, needing the distraction of idle conversation.

"As well as can be expected this early on. At least we aren't distracted by unnecessary drama."

She smiled knowingly, certain the Headmaster was referring to her fraternization with Sir during her training. Master Coen added with a charming smile, "Best thing that ever happened was you settling down so the world could continue."

"And yet I always find myself back here."

"Troublemaker to the core."

She laughed, but was unsure if he partially meant it. "How are your personal submissives doing?"

"We've added a third to the mix—seems to be the perfect combination of personalities."

"Three?" she asked in surprise. "I guess you're well on your way to a harem."

He sat back in his chair. "I would have no complaints about that, as long as my girls all get along. The real skill is recognizing who would be an asset and who would just bring chaos to our home."

"I suppose you would never have considered me a good fit, then."

"No," he agreed. "You invite chaos to the most stable of institutions."

She ignored his cheeky insult. "I assume we are still filming a spanking scene today."

He nodded, with a glint in his eye. "Yes. I noticed you were lacking a spanking scene in your first documentary."

"That I was."

"Well, today I plan to educate the American public on the pleasures of spanking." He got up from Sir's desk and held the door open for her. "My newest submissive will be joining us on the stage in a few minutes."

So it was to be in the auditorium? Brie felt honored that Master Coen was giving the world a glimpse into the heart of the Center itself.

While Brie readied her camera, she watched the Headmaster set a scene reminiscent of the one he'd done with her during training. With arms of muscular steel, Master Coen lifted the teacher's desk and set it on the stage. He returned with a chalk board and props, including a ruler, a container of pencils and an apple. He placed them carefully on the desk, taking obvious pride in setting up the scene.

"Do you have enough light, Miss Bennett?"

She shook her head. "If we could turn them up a bit, that would be optimal."

He went to the back of the auditorium and turned them up until the stage was bathed in bright light. "Enough?"

She looked through her viewfinder and gave him a thumbs-up. "Perfect."

He pulled out his cell phone to call his sub. "Meet me at the auditorium doors." While they waited, he explained to Brie, "I want you to capture the expressions on her face."

"I was thinking the same thing," she agreed. "I've set up the camera at this angle so it will center on her face and the swing of your hand. It will also allow you to strip her ass bare if you need to without exposing her nakedness."

He took a peek through the viewfinder. "Excellent, Miss Bennett."

There was a soft knock. Master Coen smiled as he walked to the door to greet his sub. A middle-aged woman entered the auditorium, dressed in a school uniform complete with knee-high socks, pigtails and a tiny little skirt. He cupped his sub's chin and kissed her before introducing her to Brie.

"Miss Bennett, I would like you to meet the newest member of my family. Her official name is raven, but we all call her rae at home. You may call her rae as well if you wish."

Brie held out her hand, admiring the woman's thick black hair. "It's a pleasure to meet you, rae. Thanks for agreeing to film with me today."

The woman shook her hand enthusiastically. "I can't believe I'm getting to be part of your film!" She turned to Master Coen. "I'm such a lucky sub."

"Yes, you are," he replied, sounding amused by her obvious excitement. His pride in her was touching to witness, but Brie had to swallow down feelings of sadness knowing Sir used to look at her the same way.

Breathe…

She played with the flower in her hair as she explained, "Just as I did in the first film, I'll stay behind the camera. Don't pay attention to it or to me. If at any time you need to stop filming, just give me the signal."

Master Coen grabbed his sub's ass with his beefy hands, pressing her against him. "Are you ready to make film history, rae?"

"Ready and willing, Master."

"Then stand next to the chalkboard and write *I will not talk when the teacher is speaking* fifty times."

Rae bowed to him before skipping up to the stage and going to the chalkboard to begin her assigned task.

"You may begin filming," Master Coen stated as he headed onto the stage to join her.

Brie followed him with the lens as Master Coen ascended the steps. She couldn't keep from smiling when he picked up the ruler from the desk and questioned, "What happens to willful students?"

Rae answered timidly, "They get punished, Headmaster."

"Yes, they do. In your case, since this is the second offense, I believe a harsher punishment is in order."

Rae stopped writing and turned to him. "Please, Headmaster, I promise to be good."

"You promised me that the last time." He hit the ruler against the desk. "Put the chalk down and lean against the desk, legs together, palms flat on the wood."

She put down the chalk hesitantly and approached the desk with a shy smile directed at him.

"Don't move," he instructed, pushing her head down on the desk so she faced the camera.

Brie felt her body respond to his forcefulness, remembering their own scene together. She hadn't really known Master Coen at that point in her training. When Brie scened with him that first time, she'd been frightened that he planned to hurt her as punishment for her involvement with Sir. Instead, the muscular trainer introduced her to the sensuality of a good spanking. It had been a surprising lesson she'd never forgotten.

Brie felt tingling sensations course down her spine as he positioned himself behind his willing sub. The Headmaster reached over and grabbed a pencil from the desk. "Open," he commanded, putting the wooden pencil near her lips. "Bite down on it. I want to be certain the other classes aren't disturbed while you take your punishment."

He took off his jacket and hung it on the chair, then unbuttoned his cuffs before slowly rolling up each sleeve to expose his impressive arms. Brie wondered how many women in America would be daydreaming of being punished by his bare hand after seeing this film.

"Ten swats to start off with." He lifted her tiny skirt and caressed her ass through the thin material of her white cotton underwear. "Young women need to learn to respect their superiors."

Rae nodded.

Brie held her breath as he swung his hand back, readying for the first swat. The distance let her know it was going to be a hard one. His hand came down on rae's right ass cheek, the sound of it echoing in the auditorium. Rae whimpered as she bit on the pencil. He delivered the second with the same force on her left ass cheek.

Rae cried out between her clenched teeth.

"Shh…" he said soothingly, rubbing her buttocks with his large hand.

Rae wiggled her ass, apparently begging for more.

He took his time, teasing her with light caresses before he finished the remaining swats. He didn't stop until all had been delivered. Rae's whimpers filled the large room, her eyes tearing up by the end.

Master Coen took the pencil from her mouth and set it on the desk. He caressed her ass gently and asked, "Why are you being punished?"

She answered sweetly, "Because I was talking in class."

"And why is that a problem?"

"You were lecturing, Headmaster."

"Yes, and I was in the middle of a very important lecture. How dare you compromise the success of other students by interrupting my lesson like that. As this is your second infraction, I can't let you off lightly."

Rae smiled, her cheek still resting on the desk. "I understand, Headmaster."

"Don't cry out."

She nodded, her eyes half-closed and glazed over with lust.

He looked at her ass and shook his head disapprovingly. "I cannot punish you properly with these on." The angle of the camera let Brie barely see the swell of her naked ass as he stripped off her panties.

"Open those legs," he commanded."

Rae adjusted her posture, keeping her cheek pressed against the wood.

"Good girl. Now let's make that ass a little pinker." He picked up the ruler and got into position. "I think another ten will do."

Rae took her punishment, moaning and gasping through it but never once crying out. The sound of wood slapping against skin was erotic, but watching rae squirm and wiggle as he applied the ruler was even sexier to Brie.

When he finally put the ruler down, both Brie and rae let out sighs. He caressed the woman's sore buttocks. "Now that's a nice shade of pink. I think you're ready for a proper spanking."

Master Coen rubbed his hands together vigorously, making them warm with friction. "I want you to count out your punishment in your prettiest voice."

Rae answered in a low, flirtatious tone, "Yes, Headmaster."

He swatted her hard, moving repeatedly from one ass cheek to the other. Rae called each one out as she had been instructed, keeping her voice light and inviting.

He stopped after twelve and leaned forward, whispering something in her ear. Then his hand disappeared between rae's legs as he nibbled on her earlobe. The soft moans she made let Brie know she was very much enjoying what Master Coen's hand was doing.

He kissed her cheek chastely before positioning himself for another round of spanking. Although rae whimpered on several occasions, she counted out each swat in the same flirtatious tone; it would allow the audience to enjoy their play. However, it was the mystery of not seeing what Master Coen's hand was doing whenever he stopped spanking that had Brie worked up.

This was an extremely naughty scene that kept an air of innocence because of the props, rae's cute little outfit and the modest camera angle. Brie hoped it would meet with Mr. Holloway's approval, even though she swore rae came at least four times during the filming.

After the scene was over, Master Coen handed his sub the apple from the desk. "To replenish your energy. I plan to ravish you in a few minutes."

Brie hurried to put her equipment away so the couple could enjoy the high they'd created together. While she was finishing up, Master Coen came over and asked, "Did you find the scene satisfactory, Miss Bennett?"

"Yes, it was…an invigorating scene."

"Rae has a fetish for spanking. Easiest way to get her off is with the bare hand," he said, looking proudly at his palm.

Brie stared at his hand, knowing its feel and allure. "You did a fine job showcasing a spanking scene, Headmaster. I especially appreciated the role-playing. I think it will read well on screen."

Rae skipped up to them. "I love playing the naughty student. Could you tell?" she asked with a grin, just before she took a big bite of her apple.

"Yes, it was quite obvious that you enjoyed it. Maybe a little *too* obvious," Brie replied with a wink.

"Spanking can get you in all kinds of delicious trouble," rae said, giving Master Coen a flirtatious bow.

That seemed to be Brie's cue to leave, so she picked up her camera bag and started towards the door. On her way out, Master Coen mentioned to her, "I suggest a visit to Nosh, the head trainer for the Dominants."

Brie turned to face him. "You think he might be interested in filming a scene?"

"It's possible."

She remembered the commanding presence of the Native American trainer during her critique of Faelan. His long hair and brown skin had been attractive to Brie, but it was his stern gaze she remembered the most.

"Nosh doesn't tolerate foolishness," Master Coen informed her.

Brie felt a pit in her stomach at the thought of meeting with him. "Is he expecting me?"

"No, but he knows of the project. I'm uncertain whether he's interested."

"Ah..."

Brie thanked Master Coen and made her way to the Dominant Training side of the school, despite her misgivings. The halls of the Training Center were empty during the day, although the business college above bustled with activity. It made for a lonely walk to the head trainer's office.

She refused to let her fear get the better of her, so she screwed up her courage, straightening her posture and throwing back her shoulders before knocking on Nosh's office door. When she heard no invitation to come in, she knocked again with a little more force. Brie was actually thrilled when she got no response. The fact was, she felt ill-prepared to face such an intimidating presence in her current emotional state.

As Brie walked to the elevator, a sense of pride washed over her. In spite of wanting to curl up and die, she had just filmed another winning scene for her documentary. Proof that she was meant to succeed in the industry, no matter what life threw at her. Still, she was anxious to get out of the Center before Nosh showed up.

She hit the elevator button several times, willing it to hurry. Naturally, that was when she heard her name being called from the commons area.

"Miss Bennett."

Confrontation

B rie closed her eyes and steeled herself before walking over to Marquis Gray. The man read her far too easily.

"You seemed in a hurry just now. Did you forget you were meeting with me?"

She avoided his eyes as she sat down, not wanting him to know she *had* forgotten his request. "I was told by the Headmaster to meet with Master Nosh. Since he isn't in his office, I had hoped the receptionist might know his whereabouts."

"Master Nosh is out for the day, so I'm afraid you will have to schedule a meeting with him later."

"Good to know." She finally met Marquis' gaze and smiled. "Then I guess we can talk if you're free now."

"Actually, I've been waiting for you. I'm growing concerned, Miss Bennett. I've invited Sir Davis to join me for dinner on several occasions, but he has yet to respond. It's not like him. Can you shed some light on the matter?"

Brie was careful with her answer, not wanting Marquis to know of their recent struggles. "Sir has been preoccupied with work lately. I'm sure it is simply an oversight."

"I thought so too, until I saw you today."

Brie groaned inwardly.

Raising an eyebrow he asked, "Are things going well?"

"As I said, Sir has been working long hours. His overseas business is beginning to take off, but it requires an inordinate amount of time."

Not a man to mince words, Marquis Gray demanded, "What's wrong? I only ask because I was your trainer and am invested in your success."

"I appreciate your concern, but it's unnecessary." Brie cursed herself when her lip trembled slightly, but was grateful that Marquis Gray didn't seem to notice.

"Why don't you invite Sir Davis for me personally, then? Saturday night. Tell him I won't accept no for an answer. You will join us as well. I know Celestia has missed your youthful presence."

Brie silently congratulated herself for successfully thwarting Marquis' intuitive powers. "I'll be happy to relay the message, Marquis Gray."

"Good. I expect to see you both at six. It appears we have much to discuss."

It was obvious that Sir was *not* anxious to meet with Marquis for dinner, although he agreed to go. As retribution, Sir made her cook an egg custard to take for dessert. She groaned as she fished out a piece of shell from the bowl of cracked eggs. The smell of vanilla, nutmeg and cinnamon was tantalizing, but she knew Marquis would never eat the dessert. She held out hope that Celestia might give her first attempt at custard a try.

Brie sprayed air deodorizer in the kitchen and down the hallway to the bedroom as the custard finished baking, just in case the smell of eggs had settled there. She knew having her make an egg dish was as much a punishment for Sir as it was for Marquis.

She was surprised Sir was uncharacteristically late picking her up that night. He did not provide her with any explanation, nor did he attempt to make up for lost time on the road.

They did not arrive at Marquis Gray's home until well after six. The door opened before they even set foot on the porch.

"I wasn't sure you were coming," Marquis told Sir, ushering Brie in with a slight smile.

"Yet here I am," Sir answered curtly, following Brie inside.

The conversation between the two Doms remained terse and formal the entire evening, a far cry from the last time they'd visited together. Luckily, Celestia was her gentle and calming self, bringing a needed sense of ease to the gathering as she took Brie's offering of dessert and directed them to seat themselves at the table.

Humorously, the first course was a Caprese salad. Brie had to stifle a giggle. Evidently both Doms thought alike. Marquis was well aware that Sir disliked tomatoes, leaving Sir to set them aside, eating only the mozzarella and basil left on his salad plate.

Marquis kept the conversation going throughout the dinner with questions about Sir's business, his trip to Japan and his future plans for his consulting business. Sir responded by peppering him with a number of questions as well. Through their discussions, Brie discovered that after her documentary released, Marquis had begun crafting custom floggers.

It seemed that a flogger handmade by the now-famous Marquis Gray was quite the 'it' item.

When the time for dessert finally came, Brie started wringing her hands under the table. Celestia brought out the covered dish and lifted the lid with a flourish.

Marquis Gray stared at the custard without any expression on his face. "Did you make this, Miss Bennett?"

"I did, Marquis Gray."

"I find myself too full to eat dessert," he announced.

"I understand."

"But I can't wait to try it," Celestia exclaimed.

Brie cut the custard pie, noting the light texture. She handed a piece to Celestia, confident it was going to be good. She then cut a small piece for herself and watched in eager anticipation as Celestia brought the dessert to her lips.

Ruby lips encased Brie's creation, but the expression on Celestia's face was not one of pleasure but of shock as she quickly swallowed and put her fork down.

Brie didn't understand and took her own bite, spitting it out immediately.

Marquis Gray picked up Celestia's plate and sniffed

it, then looked it over carefully, appearing amused. "Perfectly cooked, correct consistency... Let me guess, someone mistook salt for sugar."

Brie let out a little whimper.

"Is that true?" Sir asked her.

Brie's bottom lip quivered when she answered him, "I'm afraid so, Sir. It's inedible."

"No, it's not that bad," Celestia insisted, picking up her fork and cutting another piece. Marquis grabbed her wrist before she could put it in her mouth, forcibly taking the utensil from her.

"I will not let you poison yourself." He addressed Brie sternly. "Did I not stress numerous times during the cooking session that you must always taste your food? No one, I repeat, *no one* should ever have to eat your mistakes."

Brie looked down in shame, then turned to Sir when he said her name. She barely had enough courage to look him in the eyes.

Sir's hard stare was chilling, but then she saw a glimmer of a smile creep across his face before he began chuckling loudly. "As if eggs weren't bad enough."

As soon as Marquis and Celestia joined in his laughter, Brie let out a sigh of relief, knowing she'd been forgiven. "I apologize for the custard. I will not make that mistake again."

"No, Miss Bennett, you will *not*," Marquis asserted.

Sir held out his arms and Brie gratefully settled into them, resting her head on his chest. "Take it easy on her, Gray. She was doing me a favor."

Sir took her chin and shook it gently back and forth.

"I knew I was getting a non-cook when I collared you, but I failed to realize how deep your ineptitude goes—incredible, simply incredible."

Brie was grateful when he kissed her on the lips. At least Sir wasn't holding her honest mistake against her.

"Now that you've had your bit of fun, Sir Davis," Marquis said, "why don't we retire to the other room and let our subs clean up? There are certain things we need to discuss."

"If you feel it is necessary," Sir replied with disdain.

"Critical."

Sir kissed Brie one more time before getting up. "Thank you for the custard, my dear. It was *exactly* what the doctor ordered."

Brie watched with concern as Sir followed Marquis into the living room.

"They'll be fine," Celestia assured her.

I'm not so certain, Brie thought as she gathered the plates.

Her worries were confirmed when she returned from the kitchen to hear Sir growl angrily, "What the hell did Brie tell you?"

She cringed at the venomous tone behind the accusation. Celestia came up beside her and wrapped an arm around her waist in support as they listened to the heated exchange.

"She said nothing, Sir Davis," Marquis Gray answered. "I only had to look at her face to know that things are not well between you."

"And how is this any of your business?"

"I was her trainer, your colleague and, I thought,

your friend. I consider you a rational man, but your current actions dispute that. I understand that you are weighed down by your mother's situation, but that should not dictate how you relate to the rest of the world."

"You know nothing about it."

"Let me be frank here. You are not the person I used to know."

Sir roared defiantly, "And you're not my father, Gray!"

"Damn it, man. You promised to care for and nurture that girl in there. Have you forgotten the vows you made in front of the entire community?"

Sir's voice had become low and ominous. "I *repeat*, this is none of your business."

"You're mistaken to think so. We are a community, Sir Davis. We look out for one another, and I see you starting to spiral out of control. I *must* do something, for both your sakes."

"You're overstepping the line, here."

Marquis' answer was confident and sure. "No, I am not. You must deal head-on with the situation concerning your mother, and include Miss Bennett in the process, or you will lose her."

"You're being over-dramatic, Gray."

"And you're a blind fool if you believe that."

"Don't throw those words around so casually with me," Sir warned. "I'm not your sub."

Marquis Gray went for the jugular. "I only suspected you were a fool when you took Miss Bennett during training, but now you're proving I was correct."

Sir spat angrily, "And you've held that single indiscretion over my head ever since."

"Your impulsive nature showed a lack of control and common sense." Marquis added in a tone of disbelief, "To think that as Headmaster you risked the Center's reputation and your position to *play* with a trainee? It was inconceivable to me."

Sir's voice dripped with acid. "Cease with the lecture, old man. I repeat, you're not my father."

"Well, someone needs to be, since you're acting like a child."

"You're sorely mistaken if you think a past indiscretion gives you the right to pry into my personal life. I won't stand for this."

"Running away, Sir Davis?" Marquis taunted. "I know that has been your *modus operandi* since you were a boy, but it doesn't work for adults. Demons don't disappear on their own. They must be faced and dealt with."

The timbre of Sir's voice was frightening when he replied, "Stop pushing me, Gray, or I will be forced to push back—and I know you better than you think."

Marquis was unmoved by the threat. "Your response highlights the depths of your spiral. As I stated before, you are not the man I once knew. No wonder Miss Bennett is floundering under your care. The answer is simple. Confront the issue with your mother, or you will destroy everything you have built, including your relationship with Miss Bennett."

"I will never forget this, Gray," Sir growled, heading back to the dining room.

Marquis' sarcastic laugh followed him. "No, I'm sure you won't, but let's hope you're man enough to take heed."

"Brie!" Sir barked.

She let out the breath she'd been holding and looked apologetically at Celestia before moving to Sir's side.

"We're leaving. Gather our things and meet me in the car." Without looking back, he marched to the front door, slamming it behind him. Brie scurried to pick up her purse and coat, while Celestia covered the custard dish and handed it to her.

Brie took it with shaking hands, a tangled mess of emotions. She froze when she felt Marquis Gray's firm grip on her shoulder.

"This was unfortunate but necessary, Miss Bennett."

She nodded, unable to speak.

"Don't run outside wildly, reflecting your Master's irrational outburst. Walk to the car with confidence. It is important that you support him through this, but do not become his emotional punching bag. You do not deserve it, and it is not what he needs from you."

She glanced up at Marquis, the lump in her throat making it difficult to speak. "Thank you, Marquis Gray."

His encouraging smile calmed her frayed emotions. "We're all forced to face our demons at some point, Miss Bennett. I believe it is part of God's plan. Whether we meet them with courage or fearful avoidance is up to the individual, but the consequences of those decisions determine the course of our lives."

She clutched the custard dish to her chest, admitting quietly, "I'm afraid for Sir."

"I trust he will come through this. He is not a weak individual."

"No, he is not," she agreed vehemently.

The car horn blared from outside.

She jumped, but took a deep breath and nodded to Marquis Gray before walking to the door and opening it. Sir required her strength. She would give it to him on her terms, because that was what he needed from her.

A Gift of Flogging

The ride home was quiet. Not filled with the raging anger she'd expected, but a brooding silence—which was worse.

Rather than disturb him, Brie sat up straight and stared ahead. *I am téa, sub and lover of Sir Thane Davis. I am his condor. I will always stand beside him, I will always love him, and I will be his strength when he falters. It is my joy to do so.*

"What did Gray tell you?" Sir snarled, breaking the silence.

She turned to him, not allowing herself to react to his hostility. "He told me to stand beside you."

"Really?" It sounded as if Sir didn't believe her, but he turned his eyes back to the road. "I can't tolerate people prying into our lives."

"I understand, Sir."

He added, "I appreciate that you did not run to him with our problems."

"We are partners. What happens between us is private."

"At least *you* understand that," he spat venomously.

"Marquis only meant well."

He growled under his breath, "As if his opinion matters to me."

Despite his protests, Brie knew very well that it *did* matter to him. Everyone respected Marquis Gray—including Sir.

Over the course of several minutes, she watched his expression change from anger to pain. Sir suddenly made a U-turn and headed for the foothills, ending up at the same place they'd gone to when he'd broken down after the initial confrontation with his mother.

It was high above the city, with an impressive view of LA. Sir got out of his Lotus and walked around to the other side, opening the door and taking her hand to help her out.

Brie took it as a positive sign.

They stood in the dark, watching the vibrant city below. Even as far up as they were, the sounds of sirens, horns blaring and dogs barking floated from below, while cars constantly moved through the congested streets as airplanes flew above their heads. The city was alive—a living, breathing entity.

Brie had grown up in a small town, but she loved LA for its diversity and promise. Great things could happen here; she still believed it.

"Seeing the Beast was unnerving, Brie. That unnaturally preserved face with its expression of superiority, still beautiful even with all the tubes. Although I've been told she's braindead, looking at her, I felt she might open her eyes at any moment."

"How did seeing her like that make you feel?"

"I wasn't prepared for the opposing emotions. I thought I was, had spent two days in Japan bracing myself for it, but seeing her…"

Brie could almost imagine the love and loss he must have felt, despite the fact that his mother had been so cruel to him. Sadly, Ruth *was* his mother, and that bond was so deep it couldn't be severed no matter what she'd done to him.

"I fully expected to be overwhelmed with emotion, but not by the one emotion that consumed me."

"What was that, Sir?"

He shocked her with his answer. "I wanted to punch that smug look off her face. A grown man shouldn't feel that way." He looked up at the night sky and sighed with frustration. "Even in that state, she has power over me. Every cruel deed, every unkind word still resonates within me.

Sir shook his head with a disgusted look on his face. "That was when I realized that all the issues in my past I'd thought I'd conquered, all the growth I'd assumed I'd made were just an illusion. I'm still that boy, standing in the doorway, helpless to stop what is about to happen as she watches my father lift the gun and end my world."

Brie wrapped her arms around Sir, laying her head against his shoulder, wishing desperately that she could take away the painful memories.

"I looked at her lying in that hospital bed, Brie, and had to fight the urge to physically choke the life out of her." He brushed his hair back, a look of resignation on his face. "And yet…"

"You still love her."

"Love is an ugly word when it's associated with that woman. My feelings are tangled in a hatred so dark it scares me." He groaned, looking up at the stars again. "I counted on having resolution with her someday—it didn't matter whether it ended well, I needed that final confrontation with her. I never realized how much I depended on it. To have it stolen from me is a loss I cannot bear. I'm left floundering like a drowning man."

"It's completely understandable," she assured him, hugging Sir tighter.

His voice broke when he admitted, "I know this should be a simple decision, Brie. She needs to die, but I find myself...struggling."

Brie took his strong hand in hers. "I stand beside you, whatever you decide."

"Being next to me is a dangerous place in my current state."

"I will not fail you."

He disengaged from her embrace. "But I will fail you."

She tried to protest, but he hushed her with his finger.

"Marquis is right. I had no business collaring you. My past makes me unfit to be your Master. I knew that, but for a moment you had me believing differently."

She refused to listen. "You followed your heart. You've always insisted that if I trust my instincts, they won't steer me wrong. It's sound advice, Sir."

He disagreed, shaking his head slowly. "Instincts and the heart are two different animals. The heart cannot be trusted."

Brie smiled, taking his hand and pressing it against her cheek. "But it led me to you, Sir."

"You could have done so much better, my dear."

She could hear the pain behind his sarcastic tone, but she shook her head in defiance of his words, still smiling at him.

"Brie, I will hurt you. Hell, I already have. I'm broken, and no amount of wishful thinking can change that. I'm not what you need."

"Sir, you have chosen a path of integrity and followed it relentlessly. I admire you, and am honored to be collared by you. I'm willing to suffer alongside you now because I see a future full of promise ahead. It will be glorious."

He cupped her chin. "You are naïve and sweet, but naivety is fragile and sweetness can quickly turn to bitterness."

"I am enhanced by you, not diminished."

He gave an amused smile, shaking her chin from side to side. "Stubborn."

"Like a condor."

He laughed out loud.

Brie wanted to follow Marquis' advice and be the strength Sir needed. With trepidation, she told him, "I have a humble suggestion concerning your mother."

He raised one eyebrow, the expression on his face turning suspicious. "Speak."

Brie forged ahead, despite her sudden misgivings. "Nothing needs to be decided now. Your mother owes you for the wrongs she's done. She can wait until you're ready."

Rather than the gratitude she'd expected, his eyes blazed with renewed anger. "I do not care for the suggestion. It was not wanted, nor is it appreciated."

It seemed all the progress she'd made had been swept away in an instant, and they walked back to the car in silence.

While Brie was sipping her morning coffee the next day, Sir's cell phone rang. She picked it up off the counter and walked over to where he was working. He took it from her without a word.

"Hello?" he said into the phone. That was the first word she'd heard since their discussion the night before.

"Why are you calling?" Sir growled, obviously not pleased with the caller's identity.

He stared at Brie briefly before replying, "It's not your right."

Sir listened intently, then flared his nostrils in anger. "Fine, I'll be joining her, then." He hung up and tossed the phone onto the table in an angry huff.

"Who was that, Sir?"

"That was the infamous Gray. He's asked to film a session with you as his partner."

"With me? But why?"

"That was exactly my question. However, his explanation has merit and I won't be the one to hinder your filming career. You should know, however, that I insisted on attending the session."

Brie shook her head, knowing how badly he wanted to avoid Marquis. "You don't need to, Sir. I'll talk to him and respectfully decline his offer."

"No, Brie, I've already agreed to watch."

She gave him a troubled look. "When is the filming supposed to take place?"

"Today, before training classes begin at the Center. He asked that you call him to go over the particulars of the scene."

"I'm sorry, Sir."

"This is not your doing. I've only agreed because I believe the opportunity is a good one for your career."

She accepted his answer, but left Sir's side feeling a little light-headed.

A scene with Marquis Gray? She hadn't been under his hand since Graduation Night…

When she called Marquis, he informed her that it would be a flogging scene—an instrument he knew she enjoyed. He also shared that he was planning to use a new flogger he'd been practicing with recently, one she might find a little intimidating.

Because of her unwavering trust in Marquis, Brie agreed to the scene, but began to have second thoughts when she entered the Training Center a few hours later with Sir.

Sir picked up on her unease and stopped her in the hallway. "If at any time you wish to end it, you have my full support."

She was grateful for his sensitivity and encouragement. "I'm sure it will go well, but I appreciate you telling me that, Sir." He nodded, resting his hand against the small of her back as he escorted her into the room.

Marquis Gray seemed pleased to see them both, but directed his attention to Sir. "We'll keep this short, Sir Davis, since time is limited for both of us."

"It's best we don't speak, then," Sir replied. "Let's waste no more time than necessary."

"Agreed." Marquis turned from Sir to ask Brie, "You understand the dynamics of the scene, yes?"

"I do, Marquis Gray, but may I see your new flogger before we begin?"

"Certainly." Marquis pulled the biggest flogger she had ever seen from out of his bag. Brie couldn't even count the number of tails on the two-handed instrument. She touched the strips of leather, feeling a sense of trepidation.

"How many tails does it have?" she asked.

"Eighty."

Brie cringed. "That many?"

"It has a real thud to it," he replied, with a glint in his eye.

She backed away from the flogger. "To be honest, I'm…a little frightened of it."

"I appreciate that you are fearful, Miss Bennett. However, trust that I will warm you up to receive its unique…sensation."

She looked over at Sir, unable to hide her concern.

"You'll be fine, Brie," Sir assured her, handing her the camera.

His assertion bolstered her resolve to continue with the filming. "It may take me a few minutes to set up, Marquis Gray."

"Not an issue, Miss Bennett. I need to set out my instruments and warm up."

She worked in silence, intent on the job at hand. It wasn't until Brie caught Marquis in motion through the camera's lens that she was hit by the fact she was really about to scene with the Master.

Although it was true she'd scened with Marquis while Sir had observed her during training, it felt completely different now that she was collared. She found herself glancing apprehensively at her Master.

"Come here," Sir ordered.

Brie walked over to him, staring hard at the floor. He took her face in both hands and gazed into her eyes.

"I want to see you enjoy this scene today. This is not just about your film. This is an opportunity to let your father see what we do and why it suits you so well. He could never watch if I were your partner, but you and I both know he has respect for Marquis Gray."

She looked at him with new understanding, agreeing with his assessment.

Sir leaned down and whispered in her ear. "I don't want you looking back at me during the scene. This is about you, Gray and the flogger."

"I understand, Sir."

Brie still felt apprehensive, but there was already a positive to doing this scene with Marquis Gray. Sir was talking to her again, and for that Brie was eternally grateful.

She checked her equipment one last time, stating regretfully, "This will have to be a static shot."

"Of course it will," Marquis answered. "It helps with

the documentary's authenticity. If the girl behind the camera is in the scene being filmed, it stands to reason there is no one else working the camera. As long as the area I blocked out is in the shot, it should be fine."

She looked through the viewfinder one more time to double check before answering. "It is, Marquis Gray."

"Then undress, and come to me."

Brie felt butterflies as she slowly removed her clothes. For the shoot, Brie and Sir had decided on a two-piece set of activewear made of a thin red material. It would allow the unhindered sensation of impact play while maintaining her modesty on camera. She folded her clothes neatly and set them on the floor, just as she had during her training sessions.

Once undressed, she turned on the camera and held up her fingers, counting down silently from three to one before walking towards Marquis. She suddenly felt shy before the ghostly white Dom with eyes that penetrated her soul. It reminded her of those first days of submissive training.

Brie fingered the white orchid in her hair nervously as she approached. Marquis nodded to her as he held out his hand, murmuring, "Remember who you are."

A sense of self-confidence flooded through her hearing his words. Yes, she did know who she was and why she was here today. Brie held her head up a little higher, her eyes brimming with renewed conviction.

"Very good," he stated, directing her to stand facing the St. Andrew's cross. He knelt down at her feet to buckle her ankles first. "On your toes," Marquis ordered.

Brie stood on tiptoes for him, taking a deep breath as

he restrained her ankles. Then the ghostly Dom stood and bound her wrists. Once she was secure, he gently moved her long curls out of the way before tying a strip of lace over her eyes.

"Like old times..." he whispered.

She smiled, knowing the audience would wonder what he'd just said to her. It was an exhilarating feeling, this private dance between them being played out before the camera.

She heard Marquis Gray move away, then Mozart filled the room. Brie sighed with contentment, loving that unique element of Marquis Gray's scenes. The next sound was of a flogger cutting the air, alerting her to the fact that he was about to begin. Instead of fear, she felt only excitement and longing. She hadn't forgotten his skill with the instrument, and neither had her body.

Brie knew the moment the tails slapped across her skin that it was the same flogger he'd used in their first scene together during training—the one that had helped her to fly for the very first time.

"Color?"

"Green, Marquis Gray."

He continued lightly stimulating her skin with the flogger, using slow, fluid movements that matched the tempo of the music. It left her back warm and her muscles relaxed when he was done.

Marquis put down the instrument and returned to her, caressing her skin with a rough material she knew well.

"Lace," Brie sighed.

"Red lace."

"I'd forgotten how good it felt."

His chuckle was low and irresistible as he moved away again. After picking up the next flogger, he informed her, "This next one will demand a little more of you."

If it had been Rytsar, Brie would have tensed. However, she knew Marquis well. There was no reason to fear him, only to anticipate…

The song changed and a more lively melody started up. It made her want to move to the music, but her restraints prevented it. Instead Brie stood on her toes, her calf muscles burning, but she relished the challenge of the pose. It kept her focused on Marquis, the position showing off the beauty of her submission in physical form.

When the new flogger made contact, Brie let out a soft moan.

"Color, Miss Bennett?"

"A lovely shade of green," she answered.

The strokes were perfectly timed to match the energetic rhythm of the classical piece. It took the sensations of the physical and transformed them into a spiritual experience, connecting the stimulation with the timeless melody, etching it in her mind.

Brie felt the first hint of subspace tugging at her, demanding that she let go.

Marquis stopped at the end of the song and returned to her side. Soft fur glided over her skin, causing a cascade of pleasant shivers.

"That feels incredible," she purred.

"Nothing like opposing stimuli to heighten sensation."

"You're a true Master."

He chuckled warmly as he continued to rub the soft fur over her arms, back and neck, drawing her into connection with him—readying her mind and body for the final experience.

"It's time to fly," he announced.

Brie's heart fluttered when he left her side. The thought of that intimidating flogger stroking her back was daunting, but Marquis' skillful guidance during the scene had Brie wanting to know its character—longing to experience its unknown touch.

The music became more dramatic, matching the mood of the finale of his scene. She heard the massive flogger cutting the air before it even made contact. The impact covered her entire back, eighty tails striking at once. It was like nothing she'd experienced before.

He stroked her again, the thud of the giant flogger taking her breath away.

"Color?"

"A brilliant shade of green."

"So you enjoy the thud of this one?"

She nodded, smiling in the direction of the camera so there would be no doubt in the minds of the audience.

"Then you have my permission to fly."

Brie's loins contracted in pleasure as Marquis began stroking her with the two-handed flogger. The large area, along with the strength of the impact, meant every lash was perfect and all-encompassing.

As the strokes he applied became harder and faster, her body began to tingle, starting at the area of impact and traveling outward to her fingers and toes. Brie lost herself in the feeling, anticipating each stroke as it came and reveling in the warm sensation that coursed through her from its impact.

Eventually everything blurred, even her connection to Marquis, as she became one with the flogger. When he paused to ask her color, Brie fought to answer, knowing he was asking for the benefit of the audience that would be watching.

She stilled herself enough to answer clearly, "Green", in case her father ever watched.

"Excellent."

The thud of the flogger began again. This time she let go and allowed herself to fly…

Brie felt hands on her and heard Marquis' deep voice, but she couldn't understand what he was saying, nor did she care. She just smiled as he released her wrists, lightly rubbing them both before releasing her ankles and doing the same.

Marquis picked her up, cradling her in his arms as he whispered intimately, "Well done, Miss Bennett."

She smiled at him drunkenly. "I like your new flogger, Marquis."

"I was confident you would."

He carried Brie over to Sir and she heard her Master say begrudgingly, "That was an impressive scene, Gray."

"Thank you, Sir Davis. I've grown quite fond of the new flogger." He handed Brie over to Sir, stating abruptly, "I'm sure you understand that due to tonight's training, I have no time for aftercare."

Marquis walked over and turned off the camera before returning to Brie. "It was a pleasure to work with you again."

She was still flying on the high he'd created and grinned. "Thank you, Marquis of the Master Flogger."

Sir said nothing as he watched Marquis leave, but once the door had shut he looked down tenderly at her and said, "Well, someone needs to look after my little flier."

He carried Brie to a large lounge chair and sat down with her still in his arms. Sir gently stroked her hair with his fingertips, creating tiny trails of tickling sensation.

"You were beautiful to watch," he said softly.

She looked up at Sir, feeling a profound sense of love. "What was it like? Watching?"

"Marquis' motion reminded me of swordplay; the way he wielded that two-handed flogger was both graceful and intense." Sir gazed down at her and asked, "Did you enjoy it as much as it appeared?"

She nodded unashamedly.

Sir muttered, almost as an afterthought, "Sometimes I forget how extraordinary you are." He crushed her against his chest, rocking her gently in his protective arms for a long time before he added, "I will consider what you said about my mother."

Marquis Gray is a cunning man, Brie thought. Somehow, by having Sir watch the scene and then forcing him to take care of her afterwards, Marquis had broken down the wall between them.

It was sobering to realize what a formidable force Marquis Gray truly was.

His Virgin

S ir surprised Brie when they arrived home that night, after filming with Marquis. "Being back in my old stomping grounds and watching your scene today has brought back many pleasant memories. I have a mind to recreate one right now. Are you game, Brie?"

Brie was quick to answer. "Always, Sir."

He picked her up amid a peal of laughter and squeals, marching her straight to the bedroom. He threw her onto the bed, staring down at her hungrily. "We will relive the taking of your virginal ass, but change it up a little."

She trembled at the thought. "Change it how, Sir?"

"I'm not your trainer and you are not my student."

"Go on," she encouraged, now *very* intrigued.

"We've just met at a party with mutual friends. I'm infatuated by that perfectly shaped ass, and after much persuading you have agreed to let me take your anal virginity. I can tell you're nervous, but you invite me to your bed anyway."

Brie bit her lip, her whole body responding to his

suggestion. "That sounds delicious, Sir."

"No names tonight. We don't want to ruin the illusion."

She nodded her agreement. "No names."

"Get into character, my dear," he commanded gently.

Brie closed her eyes, imagining the thrill and excitement of bringing a stranger to her bed. The girl she was imagining had been without a partner for so long that she was nervous about being intimate with such a handsome and captivating man. Naturally, she was hesitant to give away such a private part of herself, but his confidence and interest in her was intoxicating. She might give him *anything* if he asked…

Brie opened her eyes and crossed her legs, nonchalantly covering her breasts with her arm so that she appeared less exposed, more modest. Gazing up at Sir, she swore he looked different—as if he were younger, less sure of himself. However, the hunger in his eyes remained, drawing her to him. It seemed Sir was every bit as good at getting into character as she was, and it thrilled her to the core.

She patted the area beside her on the bed, beseeching him to join her.

He smiled down at Brie as he meticulously unbuttoned his shirt and casually cast it to the floor. She held her breath when he lay next to her, suddenly feeling unsure of herself.

He cupped her chin gently and kissed her—and all uncertainty melted away. His kiss was demanding, yet tender at the same time. When he pulled away, she sighed with contentment. Without asking, he took her wrist and moved her arm to her side so he could stare unimpeded at her breasts. Her nipples hardened under the material of her blouse because of his intense scrutiny.

She held her breath when his finger lightly grazed her erect nipple, sending wavelets of energy down to her groin. She moaned into her pillow, wondering what kind of power he possessed.

"How long has it been?"

Brie laughed in disbelief. "You don't ask a girl a question like that. It's considered rude."

He continued to lightly play with her nipples as he replied, "I only asked to gauge how I should proceed with you."

She pursed her lips, embarrassed to admit the truth. "A year and three months…and five days."

He gave her a charming half-grin. "Such an exact answer."

"Yeah, so it's been a while," she replied, in a voice that didn't invite any more questions or comments on the subject.

He circled her nipple lazily with his finger, looking rather amused. "Then I suppose I should take it slow with you."

"As opposed to?"

"As opposed to turning you over right now, holding you down, ripping your clothes off and fucking that sweet little ass."

Her pussy contracted with pleasure as she imagined him on top of her, pumping his cock into her, but she definitely wasn't ready to be ravished like that—at least not yet.

"Slow is nice," she agreed.

He took her hand and moved it down so she could feel his growing erection. She swallowed nervously, shocked that she was really going let a stranger fuck her but excited by the prospect.

She bit her lip in concentration as she caressed and squeezed his hard cock, while his hand traveled to her ass and cupped her butt cheek. "I think we need you out of these clothes."

She quickly ripped off her shirt and removed her bra, tossing them onto the nightstand. He pushed her down gently and unbuttoned her jeans, slowly pulling them off along with her panties. Then he stared at her.

She shivered under his admiring gaze, unused to such attention. When she tried to cover herself, he slowly shook his head. She couldn't help smiling as she relaxed her arms and let him stare freely at her body.

This perfect man lay with her again, nibbling her ear as he grabbed her ass. "There's something about un-touched territory that is so damn sexy to me."

She stiffened in his arms when she felt him lightly rim her anus with his finger. Brie vividly remembered when Sir had taken her that first time. She'd been fearful but too turned on to deny him. That moment when his cock had breached her virginal ass was something she'd never forgotten. And now she was getting to relive it again with Sir.

"Don't be afraid," he whispered.

Just him saying that made her heart race.

He slowly turned her over onto her stomach and

proceeded to caress her bare bottom. "Such a perfect ass. The shape, the feel of it in my hands…"

She moaned into her pillow again, still anxious but charmed by his praise.

He leaned over and kissed her on the lips, exploring her mouth with his tongue as his fingers caressed and teased her pussy, which was getting wetter by the second. He rubbed her clit, increasing her excitement, and just when she thought she couldn't take any more, he moved his hand lower, pressing his finger against her tight rosette.

She gasped softly, her body resisting the invasion as his finger slowly slipped inside. The feel of it was totally foreign, naughty and unsettling—and she froze.

His kisses became more passionate as he distracted her with his tongue while his finger sought even deeper access.

"Relax…" He took her by the waist and rolled her on top of him, continuing the deep kisses as his hand traveled back to finger her ass.

She gazed into his eyes as they kissed. Those mesmerizing eyes called to her, urging her to submit to his need. Although she was curious to know the feel of a man inside her in this extremely intimate way, the truth was, she also wanted to be possessed, to abandon herself completely to his carnal needs.

Between kisses, she whispered, "I'm yours."

He grunted in response, rolling her back onto the bed so he could unbutton his pants. He removed his clothes, throwing them off the bed.

She couldn't help staring at the stranger before her.

The hair on his well-built chest complemented the dark pubic hair that framed the most handsome cock she'd ever seen. If a girl was going to give away her virginity, that cock was definitely worthy to take it.

"Where's your lubricant?"

She blushed. The question made what they were about to do that much more real. She giggled nervously, pointing to the nightstand.

He reached over and opened the drawer to retrieve it. "Give me your hand."

She held it out for him and he squeezed a coin-sized amount into her palm. He then pressed her hand to his cock. "Rub it all over."

Her heart skipped a beat when she touched his naked shaft for the first time. It was rock hard, but the head was smooth and kissable. Before she covered it in lubricant, Brie leaned over and kissed the tip. It twitched in response, obviously liking her attention.

She wrapped her hand around the length of him and began an up-and-down motion as she coated him with the slippery substance. He placed his hand over hers and forced her to squeeze harder. "Like that," he instructed.

It was so sexy being directed how to please him. Normally guys left her guessing and she could only hope she was doing a good job.

He took his hand away from her and watched as she continued to stroke him, covering the head of his shaft all the way down to the base with the clear, odorless gel. After she was done, he put a small amount on two of his own fingers. He rubbed the gel between them with his thumb, then scooted next to her, reaching around to play with her ass.

She bit her lip as he coated the outside of her sensitive area with the lube, then slipped his finger back inside. Just like the first time, her body resisted the infiltration. He kissed her again, his probing tongue demanding her full attention. Tingles of fear coursed through her as he pushed a second finger inside her, stretching her taut muscles.

"Oh God, your ass is tight," he growled lustfully.

She whimpered into his mouth, aroused by this naughty thing they were doing. Knowing how excited and turned on he was made the act that much more exhilarating.

Her loins contracted with fearful pleasure when he instructed her to get on her hands and knees. She did as he'd asked, but it seemed surreal when she felt the bed shift as he positioned himself behind her, grabbing onto her waist.

"No other man will feel what I am about to feel."

She let out a nervous sigh. He was right. She was giving this stranger a part of herself no one else had known. It was both thrilling and disconcerting. He massaged her ass with both hands, relaxing her body as he prolonged the moment of penetration. She stiffened when she felt his cock settle in the valley of her ass cheeks.

Brie didn't realize she'd stopped breathing until he said, "Don't hold your breath. It tenses the body."

She let out it out, whispering apologetically, "Sorry."

"I can empathize—this is a singular moment."

He wrapped one hand around her throat and pulled her head back to kiss her, pressing his hard shaft against her taut hole.

She cried out when her body opened for him and his cock slipped into her ass. "Nice," he murmured as he gently thrust.

Brie closed her eyes, concentrating on the fullness of his shaft. Being taken this way felt completely different from being taken vaginally. The sensitivity and tightness was intoxicating, but she was unsure how much of his cock she could take.

"Please be gentle."

"Of course," he assured her as he tightened his grip on her throat, "but you are taking all of me tonight."

A feeling of reckless abandon washed over her.

He was in control.

She lifted her chin towards him and was rewarded with the feel of his warm lips on hers. His thrusting became more pronounced as his shaft pushed farther in, stretching her achingly. The guttural noises he made as he fucked her turned her on even more.

Of all the men she'd known, he was the first to make her feel this way—wicked and dangerously sexy.

He let go of her throat, placing his hands on her hips for more leverage. His thrusts became even deeper, demanding she relax to take all of him, but he kept the rhythm slow and easy. It was as if he were making love to her.

She soaked in the sensations, embracing the resistance, the deepness of his penetration and the feeling of utter possession. She was his in that moment.

She looked back and watched his face as he fucked her ass, a look of impassioned hunger in his eyes. She wondered what he was thinking, what he was playing out in his mind as he took her.

"You're so tight, I don't think I can last much longer," he announced.

Knowing her body was such a turn-on to him heightened her own arousal and she wasn't ready for it to end. "Don't stop," she begged.

He lowered himself, wrapping his arms around her as he grunted into her ear. "I want you to come for me."

She whimpered as he changed the angle of thrust and hit a new area of stimulation. It slowly built as he rolled his hips in measured, rhythmic motions.

The feeling soon became overwhelming, but she fought against it, wanting her climax to build until it exploded with power. That was when he bit her neck and all reason left her.

She arched her back, inviting deeper access as her body convulsed with delicious release. He murmured huskily, "That's it, virgin, come for me."

She was speechless, her whole body shuddering after the climax had passed, completely spent by the passion and emotion behind the act.

"And now it's my turn…"

He lifted himself up and placed his hands on her shoulders, pushing his shaft so deep inside her that she gasped.

"My come is going to bathe your virginal ass."

She held her breath so she wouldn't miss a second of the experience. He didn't move a muscle as he orgasmed. Brie felt the pulsing of his manhood and the rhythmic release of his warm seed inside her.

Sir's low, subtle cries of passion took her back to their first night together—the night he'd claimed her anal virginity and her heart. The night he'd exposed that vulnerable side of himself for the briefest of moments.

As he lowered himself onto her now, with his shaft still buried deep inside, Brie reflected on how far they'd come. Sir nuzzled her neck, wrapping his arms back around her to hold her tight.

Condors forever...

Magic in the Air

Even though it didn't feel like Christmas, with sunshine and warm weather, Brie couldn't wait to celebrate her first Christmas with Sir.

"I just love Christmas, Sir! All the decorations, the cookies, the Christmas carols…stockings hung on the mantel, wrapped presents with bows, all made complete with a twinkling tree." She sighed contentedly. "Nothing beats the magic of Christmas."

He looked at her somberly. "I hate to tell you this, Brie, but I don't do Christmas."

Her smile faltered. "What do you mean, you don't *do* Christmas?"

"The holiday is meant for children. I put away childish things long ago."

She tried to hide her severe disappointment. "Not even a tree?"

"No. Look around this place. A dying tree would only disrupt the aesthetics of our home."

Even though she preferred real trees, she offered, "Why don't we get an artificial one? That way it won't drop needles on the marble."

"That's not the point. It would be an eyesore."

She could tell by the tone of his voice that he would not entertain a tree no matter how much she begged. "Can I at least hang up twinkling lights?"

"Brie," he glanced around the apartment for emphasis, "Christmas lights would take away from the calm serenity I have created here. I prefer things the way they are."

Her hopes dashed, she replied unenthusiastically, "Only if it pleases you, Sir."

Sir put his hand on her head. "Sorry to disappoint you, my dear, but I prefer to work through the holidays. It gives me an edge over the competition. While others take off two weeks at the end of the year, I burn the midnight oil. I suggest you do the same."

Brie sighed in resignation. "I can see how it's a sensible choice, Sir, but it doesn't seem very...fun."

"Life isn't all fun and games, babygirl. Surely you understand that."

"I do," she said in a lackluster voice.

"Do I need to remind you that you partnered with a man, not a little boy?"

She looked up into his magnetic eyes and smiled boldly, unwilling to give up just yet. "Still, Sir, I would like to get to know that little boy."

He shook his head. "That boy died long ago. Best if you get that notion out of your head."

"What about a candle, Sir?" she pressed.

He glared at her, but she met his gaze bravely. Finally, he rolled his eyes. "Fine. One candle—pine scented so you can satisfy your need for a tree."

Brie felt a sense of victory, but hid it by lowering her head and stating humbly, "Thank you, Sir."

"Bah, humbug," he said, retiring to his desk, but she detected a hint of amusement in his voice.

Brie was grateful that Sir was allowing her the small privilege of a candle. It gave her hope that he would not be angry when she presented him with her Christmas present. Whether he *did* Christmas or not, giving a present on Christmas morning was important to her. More than he could ever know.

Brie waited in the notorious—at least to her—Room forty-two at the Submissive Training Center. Marquis Gray had set up the arrangements, fully supportive of her choice of a Christmas gift for Sir. He'd declined to assist her, due to time issues, but had assured her that his replacement would do an exceptional job. She was extremely anxious about meeting the person Marquis felt worthy to instruct her.

She heard manly footsteps approaching and held her breath as the door opened. The impressive male who walked into the room had Brie grinning from ear to ear.

"Boa!"

"Hello, Brie."

"I had no idea you were a chef!"

"I'm not classically trained, but I've worked in a restaurant." He shut the door behind him and handed her one of the aprons he was holding. "I was told we're limited to short lessons, so let's get started."

"Sounds great." As she put on her apron, she asked, "Did you run your own restaurant?"

"No, I was a sous chef. I actually met my Mistress there."

"Oh, do tell," Brie encouraged.

"Not until I test your cooking skills."

She looked at him apologetically. "I don't have any. Didn't Marquis tell you?"

He chuckled. "I'd like to see for myself. Let's make it something simple. Prepare parmesan noodles for me."

"Like just noodles, some butter and cheese?"

"Sure."

Boa stood beside the cooking station and asked her to begin. Brie took a deep breath before leaving him to search the pantry for the needed ingredients. Once she'd found the spaghetti noodles, she grabbed a stick of butter and a shaker of parmesan cheese.

His eyes followed her every movement in the kitchen, making even simple things like filling up the pot with water a little intimidating. To pass the time while she waited for the water to boil, she cut the stick of butter into tiny pieces, hoping it would impress him. Then she stood and watched the pot, silently willing it to boil faster.

"So, Boa, where did you learn to cook Italian food?"

"When I was a senior in high school, I transferred to Italy for a semester. It was there I learned my passion for cooking, and the importance of simple ingredients."

"You believe you can really teach me how to make

Sir's favorite dish?"

"I have no doubt."

She said dreamily, "All I want on Christmas morning is to see Sir eat my *ribollita* and say 'It reminds me of my fathers'." Tears came to her eyes just thinking about it.

"I don't know if we can get him to say those exact words, but your dish will taste authentic."

Brie smiled at Boa. "That's all I ask."

When the rolling bubbles started, she took the dried pasta and broke it in half to fit in the pot. She set the timer to ten minutes and minced the butter into even finer pieces.

When the timer went off, she took the pot off the stove and strained the noodles. Taking out a separate bowl, she threw the cooked pasta inside and sprinkled the tiny pieces of butter on top. Happily, it didn't take long to melt when she stirred it.

She portioned out a bowl for him to taste and shook a layer of parmesan cheese on top. It looked really bland, so she ran to the pantry and grabbed some parsley, throwing it in the bowl.

Brie smiled nervously as she handed the steaming pasta to Boa. "*Bon appetit.*"

He removed the parsley, stating, "Totally unnecessary." He then took his fork and twisted several noodles onto it, staring at the forkful briefly before tasting it. He chewed it for several seconds before swallowing. "Do you normally cook pasta for Sir Davis?"

"He prefers to cook that himself."

"I'm not surprised."

She smiled sadly. "I did warn you that I have no

skills."

"Let me first go over your choices for the dish. Although I can understand why you chose dried noodles based on your limited skills, I have to wonder why you didn't salt the water. Your noodles lack flavor."

"I thought salting the water was supposed to make it boil faster, which I've heard is untrue."

"You salt the water to give your noodles taste."

She blushed. "Ah…"

"I also noticed that you relied on the timer to determine whether they were done. Do you know of any other method?"

"Well, I've heard of people throwing the pasta at the wall to see if it sticks, but that seems a little silly to me."

He laughed. "Unless you like your walls covered in starch and your noodles overcooked, I don't recommend it."

"So how *do* you get perfectly cooked noodles?"

"It's a closely guarded secret, but I will share it with you." He motioned her close, as if he was going to tell her a coveted secret. Brie leaned in eagerly and heard, "You taste them."

She snorted. "Very funny, Boa."

"I'm completely serious. You take one out and taste it. If it has an undercooked texture, wait a little longer. If it's mushy, throw the batch out and start again. While you can use a timer for guidance, you should never serve noodles you haven't sampled first."

He handed her a fork. "So taste the ones you served me and tell me what you think."

She twirled the noodles onto her fork and took a

bite. Two noodles were stuck together and almost crunchy in texture. "Undercooked?"

"No. You failed to stir the pot, so they stuck together. Personally, I wouldn't eat this if you paid me."

"So you want me to start again?"

"No, I want to teach you how to make fresh pasta. Your Master should never have to eat dried noodles. It's a waste of calories."

Boa gathered flour, eggs, salt, a clove of garlic, oil olive and a wedge of parmesan cheese and set them before her. "Simple, fresh ingredients."

He piled up a mound of flour on the cutting board and made a well in the center. He cracked in the eggs, sprinkled a little salt and added some olive oil. Then, with his bare hands, he began to mix the ingredients.

While he mixed and kneaded the dough, he asked if she had any questions.

"Personal or cooking-related?"

"Either."

"You said you met your Mistress at a restaurant. What's the story?"

Boa's eyes twinkled when he shared. "Mistress came to eat at the place I worked. She raved about the appetizer she'd had, and asked to see the chef." He shrugged. "It happened to be the only dish of mine that my boss allowed on the menu. When she realized the chef hadn't created it, she insisted on meeting me."

"And that was the beginning of you two?"

He chuckled. "Actually, it took a bit of convincing on her part. You see, I considered myself a manly man at the time. Took a while for Mistress to introduce me to my more submissive side."

He put his muscle into the kneading of the dough, moving with a fluid, thrusting motion. The movement was almost sexual in nature. She took a peek at his crotch area and noticed a very large bulge.

"You really get into cooking, don't you?" she commented.

"Yes. I think that's why I never made it past sous chef. I intimidated the other men in the kitchen with my passion for cooking."

Glancing at his bulge again, Brie thought to herself, *That's not the only thing that intimidated them.*

"Normally you let the dough rest for an hour, but I will just roll it out because of the limited time."

Boa got out a small manual pasta machine and rolled the dough through it several times, making it thinner with each pass. Then he changed the setting and cut it into thin strips.

"It takes a lot less time for fresh pasta to cook." He separated the noodles as he put them in the salted water and stirred it. While it boiled, he put some olive oil in a small sauté pan and used a garlic press to add several cloves of garlic to the oil. A minute later he pulled it from the heat, strained the noodles and put them in a large bowl. He drizzled the heated oil over them, added the parmesan and tossed the noodles lightly.

Boa handed her a fork and they both served themselves from the serving bowl. He added a final sprinkling of cheese, stating apologetically, "The pasta would be lighter if it had time to rest."

She took a bite and purred. Such simple ingredients,

but the texture of the noodles along with the tang of olive oil and toasted garlic was amazing. "I can make this?"

"Of course, you saw how easy it was."

She laughed. "Marquis makes omelets look easy— that doesn't mean they are."

Boa patted her on the shoulder. "By the time I'm done with you, you'll have several Italian dishes under your belt that I guarantee your Master will enjoy."

He looked up at the clock. "Looks like we're out of time here."

After they'd cleaned up the kitchen, Boa escorted her to the school entrance. "So what does your Master think you're doing right now?"

"I told him I'm using the Center's resources to work on my documentary for the next two weeks, which is totally true. I just haven't mentioned the extra time for cooking lessons."

"Oh, the hoops a sub must jump through in order to surprise her Master."

She grinned. "It's not easy, I tell ya."

He winked as she walked through the door. "Until tomorrow, then."

Brie was in for her own surprise on Christmas Eve. She came home to find Sir standing in the hallway waiting for her—a mischievous smirk on his face.

"What's up?" she asked cautiously, putting her camera equipment down.

He nodded his head towards the coffee table. Brie gasped when she saw what was sitting on it. She approached the tiny Christmas tree, squealing with delight.

"I won't have dead things in my home, but I have no objection to a living piece of art."

Brie stared in awe at the miniature tree, perfect in every way.

"It's a twenty-six year old Christmas bonsai," he explained.

She shook her head in amazement. "It looks exactly like a full-grown pine tree, only in miniature form." She stroked the delicate limbs. "It's like a little miracle."

"I'm glad you like it."

She stood up and hugged him. "I love it, Sir!"

"I enquired and was told that you can put miniature lights on it without harming the tree." He took a box of tiny lights out of his pocket and handed it to her.

She looked up at him, bursting with joy. "Thank you, from the bottom of my heart, Sir." She bit her lip and said, "I bought you a little something, too. Can I get it, Sir?"

"It's not a present, is it?"

"Oh no, Sir. It's just something to get you in the mood."

He raised an eyebrow. "In the mood, you say? Then you have my permission to get it."

She ran to the bedroom, quickly retrieving her wrapped gift from the closet.

Brie walked back to him and knelt at his feet, trying hard to hide the silly grin on her face as she handed over the gift.

"I thought you said it wasn't a present," Sir admonished.

She shook her head and peeked up at him. "It's not, Sir. I just like wrapping things at this time of year." She watched with bated breath as he unwrapped her gift. He pulled it from the paper and looked at it oddly.

"It's a Santa hat, Sir."

"I can see that."

"May I have it?" she asked.

He handed it to her.

Brie rocked off her heels and placed it on his head, adjusting it to a charming angle and moving the fuzzy ball to the side. She stood back to admire how adorable he looked. "It's perfect!"

He tilted his head, frowning. "Seriously, Brie."

It made him looked even more adorable, and she beamed with delight. "You make a stern, wise old Santa, Sir."

"Wise?"

She covered her mouth.

"Come here," he said, sitting down and pointing to his lap.

She was feeling particularly naughty and blurted, "If I lie on your lap, can I tell you what I want for Christmas?"

He gazed at her sternly, shaking his head as he pointed again to his muscular thighs.

Brie took a deep breath before lying down. He lifted her little red kilt and rubbed his hand over her ass. "This *wise* old Santa will show no mercy tonight."

With that, he swatted her ass hard enough that the sound of it echoed through the quiet apartment. She cried out in surprise at the power behind his hand, then giggled.

"Oh, my goodness, that hurt!"

Another, equally forceful swat followed. The sting of it radiated from the area of contact and the electricity of it traveled straight to her pussy.

How did he do that?

Spankings never felt as good as when Sir delivered them—even Headmaster Coen's skill did not compare. She gasped as he continued to spank her naughty little ass, bringing tears to her eyes while making her equally wet with desire.

When he finally stopped, she squeaked, trembling on his lap.

"Do you have anything to say?"

"I'm sorry for my disrespect, Sir. I did not mean to call you wise."

He swatted her with extra force.

She squeaked. "What was that for?"

"Willful misrepresentation. You led me to believe this item would get me in the mood."

Brie smiled up at him, her ass still stinging from his hand. "I meant in the mood for Christmas, Sir."

He gave her a crooked smile, chuckling in disbelief at her brashness. "You are a naughty girl, Brie Bennett."

"Speaking of naughty, I've always fantasized about eating Santa."

He looked properly shocked. "You *are* wicked."

Sir took off the hat and placed it on the coffee table

before lifting her off his lap and ordering her to strip. Brie smiled as she slipped off her panties and flirtatiously flipped her little red kilt, letting him catch a glimpse of her bare mound.

"Very nice."

Giving him a curtsy, she turned away and slowly unzipped the kilt, letting it fall to the floor. She pulled off her blouse next, wiggling her hips as she did, so that he could admire her red little ass. Brie undid her lacy bra and flung it behind her, impressed when he deftly caught it in his hand.

She turned to face him again and presented herself, hands behind her back, her legs slightly spread where she stood to show her willingness for play.

Sir unbuttoned his slacks and smiled lewdly. "Come and put those naughty lips around this cock."

Brie sauntered up to him and gratefully sank to the floor, opening her mouth to take his manhood, but Sir stopped her. "Wait."

He retrieved the hat from the coffee table and placed it on her head. "Begin."

She smiled up at him, the soft furry ball of the hat tickling her cheek. Brie opened her lips and took his shaft into her mouth, purring as she flicked and licked the head of it. The tanginess of his pre-come played on her tongue. Tasting his excitement always had an erotic effect on her, making her pussy ache to satisfy his manly desire.

When he took her head in his hands and guided her deeper onto his shaft, she moaned in pure bliss.

"Remember the first time you took my cock in your

mouth?"

She pulled away to answer him, smiling sweetly. "Of course I do, Sir."

"As I recall, you had to have your hands tied behind your back, but look at you now..." He guided her back onto his cock and she relaxed her throat to take him deep. She swallowed the length of his shaft, then slowly pulled back before returning to the base in short, slow movements. It was the same move she'd used when she'd deep-throated him for the first time.

The motion helped to constrict her throat, giving him the tightness he enjoyed. It also left her in control, allowing her to lavish love on his cock at her own pace.

Sir surprised her by holding her head against him for several moments before releasing her. It forced her to quiet herself as she felt her heart start pounding from the temporary lack of oxygen.

Brie took in several deep breaths before eagerly taking him again, excited by the power play. She rode up and down his shaft until he held her still, her lips buried in his dark pubic hair.

He took longer to release her this time, forcing her to concentrate on him. "Next time, I will come," he informed her as she pulled away.

She shivered with anticipation, taking long, deep breaths to ready herself for the challenge. She wiped her mouth with a playful smile. Oral sex had a way of making both partners powerful at the same time. She knew he struggled not to come as she deep-throated him, and he knew he had complete control of her mouth. It was an exciting exchange between Dominant and submissive.

She nibbled and teased the head of his shaft with her teeth and tongue, drawing out his final release. The fact that Sir allowed it meant that he was enjoying the anticipation as much as she.

Taking one last deep breath, she opened her lips wide and took his rock-hard shaft into her mouth. Sir groaned as his cock traveled down her tight throat. He held her head in place against him, then began thrusting slowly.

His build-up was slow, forcing her to be patient and to trust him as her heart pounded and her lungs burned. But then the moment came, the swelling of his cock just before the rhythmic release of his seed. Both groaned in ecstasy as his come shot down her throat—the exchange complete.

"I'm not done with you yet, naughty girl."

Brie giggled as he picked her up and slung her over his shoulder, slapping her ass hard before carrying her towards the bedroom.

Christmas Kink

Brie woke up early on Christmas morning and tried to roll out of bed without waking Sir, but he wrapped his arm tightly around her. "Where are you going at four in the morning?"

"You gave me permission last night, Sir. Remember, it's a surprise. Go back to sleep."

He took his arm away. "Fine, leave your Master cold and alone."

She leaned over and kissed his cheek. "You'll thank me later, I promise."

"I can't imagine anything can equal your warm body pressed against mine."

Brie smiled as she tiptoed out of the room, closing the door quietly behind her. She hurried to the kitchen, hardly able to contain her excitement. She put on a frilly apron to protect her naked body as she cooked, and laid out the tools required for the dish.

For the first time in her life, Brie felt confident in the kitchen, knowing exactly what she needed to do to create the special dish Sir loved. She put on headphones and turned up the volume, dancing and twirling to Christmas music as she cooked.

Every ingredient was professionally and lovingly handled as she recreated the *ribollita*. She thought of Sir's father making this dish for his family, and could relate to the love and joy he must have felt. She was grateful for that love, even though it had ended in tragedy, because Sir was a direct result.

She thought back to her own childhood, remembering with fondness the excitement of Christmas morning. She'd wake up far too early, waiting for sounds of her parents. Her father never failed to awaken at an ungodly hour, as excited as she was for the magic of Christmas to begin. Before she was allowed to unwrap presents, however, they would have hot chocolate together as a family—a special cocoa that was reserved only for Christmas morning. The three of them would spend that time reminiscing about their best and worst Christmas memories.

Brie suddenly had an image of Ruth. Instead of lying in a hospital bed covered in tubes, she was a young mother in love. *I bet you giggled on Christmas morning when your little boy got up and raced to the tree to discover what Santa had brought for him.*

A tear escaped, but Brie brushed it away. Christmas morning was not a time for crying. She smiled instead as she put the final touches on the dish and waited for Sir. Luckily, her wait was not long.

"What's this I smell?" Sir asked as he walked down the hallway towards her.

Brie quickly took off her apron and earphones. She

took a proper stance as she waited for him, her heart racing with excitement. When he rounded the corner, she directed him to sit at the kitchen table, which she had already set with red napkins, gold bowls and a small poinsettia as the centerpiece.

She explained, "When I was a girl, we would always come to the table early on Christmas morning for hot chocolate. I thought it would be nice if we changed the tradition a little." With nerves threatening to do her in, she took the large pot from the stove and placed it before Sir. She took a deep breath before lifting the lid and presenting it to him.

He stared at her dish with a look of astonishment. "Is this what I think it is?"

She nodded eagerly, grabbing olive oil and freshly grated parmesan cheese and placing them on the table.

"Did you make it?"

Again she nodded vigorously.

"All by yourself?"

"It's my gift to you."

"It smells delicious." He spooned a healthy amount into his bowl and drizzled olive oil over it, adding the parmesan last.

Brie couldn't breathe as she waited for him to take a bite, clasping her hands against her chest as she watched. She stared at his luscious lips as he blew on the spoon before taking that first taste. Her gaze traveled up to his eyes and she was surprised to see that they were watering.

"Is it not good enough, Sir?"

"It's perfection, Brie."

She felt as if she was going to burst with happiness. "I'm so glad, Sir."

He took another spoonful and asked her to taste it. As she swallowed the savory Italian stew, he told her, "You are tasting my childhood."

She looked at him gratefully. "Thank you, Sir. I'm honored you feel that way."

"No, thank *you*, Brie. I cannot think of a more fitting Christmas gift."

He took her in his lap and the two of them shared his bowl. It was the most romantic thing ever.

When he was done, he kissed her on the lips. "I told you that I don't do the whole Christmas scene."

"I know, Sir. That's okay. It's the giving part I like the most, anyway."

He smiled knowingly. "That doesn't surprise me, little sub."

She grinned at him, laying her head on his shoulder.

"However…" He slipped a small red envelope onto the table.

Her eyes widened as she took it. "What's this?"

"Open it and find out."

She hurriedly ripped the tiny envelope open, pulling out a handwritten note in Sir's exquisite penmanship.

Many people decorate for Christmas.

Open the front door to retrieve my favorite kind of decoration.

Brie looked at him questioningly. "Sir?"

He said nothing, waiting for her to follow his instructions.

Brie went up to the door and looked through the peephole, not seeing anything or anyone. Completely naked, she unlocked the front door and opened it a crack. The hallway was silent because of the earliness of the hour.

She opened the door a little wider and squealed with joy when she spied a large plastic candy cane leaning against the wall.

Brie grabbed it, noticing there was a note attached. She quickly shut the door and opened it.

> Return the cane to its owner and proceed to
> your reflection.

Brie ran back to Sir, tickled by his little scavenger hunt.

She formally held out the decorative cane with both hands. He took it from her and placed it on the table. She thought she knew where to head next, and ran down the hallway towards the bathroom, giggling like a little girl. On the counter she found two snowflake ornaments trimmed in gold, with clips to attach them to the tree. She wondered whether they represented the two of them, and gave each a kiss before reading her next note.

> Return the ornaments and explore my place of work
> to find your next surprise.

She was curious what the next one might be as she handed Sir the beautiful snowflakes. "They're so pretty, Sir."

He had a definite smirk on his face when he placed them on the table.

Brie went to his desk, expecting to see a gift waiting for her, but it was as clean and tidy as it always was. She looked at her note again and realized he'd instructed her to explore the area.

She started opening all the drawers, a sense of excitement building as she searched for her surprise. Inside the bottom drawer, she found a spool of thick velvet ribbon. She took it out along with another note.

Return my ribbon and find the stick of mint where food is stored.

She walked back to Sir and handed him the ribbon, which he carefully put beside the other items. Brie disappeared into the pantry next, but second-guessed herself when she couldn't find anything. Surely it had to be the place he meant. She searched again, being more thorough, and was rewarded when she found a huge peppermint stick hidden amongst the dried herbs.

Brie gazed at the unusually large candy, wondering where Sir had purchased it. The thought of him spending time and energy finding these unique gifts for her was humbling and sweet. She read the note attached with a sense of deep appreciation.

Return my peppermint stick and go to the room that gets the least use to find something that twinkles.

She came out of the pantry with both hands wrapped around the thick peppermint stick, and handed it to him.

She noticed the sparkle in his eye and suspected she knew where it might be going later.

Brie skipped down the hall and opened the door to the spare room. Sir was right; it rarely got any action, having become a makeshift storage room for the things she hadn't been willing to part with, but never used.

She had a much harder time finding the gift because of all the places it could be hidden. She checked under the bed, in all the dresser drawers, and then headed to the closet. Up on the highest shelf she found what she was looking for—two boxes of LED Christmas lights, one red set and one white. She pressed them against her chest. Sir knew her love of twinkling lights. She pulled out the note from the envelope, smiling like a fool.

Return the lights and head to your favorite spot after a long day apart.

She skipped back to him and knelt, handing him both boxes. "Thank you, Sir."

"You are not done yet, little sub."

She looked up at him. "I hope you know what this means to me." She rocked off her heels gracefully and hugged him before heading off to her next surprise.

The first spot she checked was the area in the hallway where she would await his return. There was nothing there, so she headed towards the couch. It was the place where she would kneel while Sir stroked her hair. Sure enough, on the floor she found sprigs of pine bundled together with a red bow. She held them up to her nose and breathed in their aromatic scent. He'd thought of everything.

Underneath the pine was another red envelope. She ripped it open and read its contents.

Return the pine and find the needed item in the storage of textiles.

She returned to her Master and handed over the pine bundle before running to the linen closet. She was rewarded with an ivory-colored hand towel sporting a candy cane pattern at the bottom. She picked up the red envelope attached to it.

Return my towel and find your next gift nestled in a safe place in the hallway.

Brie grinned when she handed the Christmas towel to Sir. He winked at her, laying it on the table. She left to look up and down the hallway, examining each painting and sculpture mounted to the wall. Nothing...

She scanned the area again, her eyes resting on his suit jacket hanging on the hook. A smile spread across her face. Bingo! She stuffed her hands into each of the pockets, finally finding her prize in the small inner breast pocket. Brie pulled out a miniature chocolate Santa wrapped in foil, along with the next red envelope. The clue was especially alluring.

Return Santa to me and find the place your fantasies lie.

Brie walked back to Sir and gave him the tiny Santa.

She bit her lip as he placed it on the table. Just what did Sir have planned with that single piece of chocolate?

"Go forth and find," he commanded.

She skipped off to the bedroom, thinking that Sir's Christmas was like Christmas on steroids.

The first place she checked was the closet. It was the place which held all the tools responsible for making her fantasies come true. But after searching through it twice, she still hadn't found anything unusual. It didn't help that Sir hadn't stated in his note what she was supposed to look for.

Sir raised his eyebrow when she returned empty-handed. She was slightly embarrassed when she admitted she couldn't find the gift.

"I'm disappointed."

Oh, that cut her to the quick. Of course he'd expected she'd know where her fantasies lay. Was it Sir? She nonchalantly peeked between his legs.

"No, Brie. Not there, but I'm flattered."

She blushed. "I *will* find it," she assured him as she headed back into the bedroom.

It had to be there—she was certain of it. Brie checked around the bed and under it before returning to the closet. This time, she checked each tool carefully in case there was a new one she'd missed.

Having had no luck, she left the closet and glanced around the room again. That was when her gaze landed on her nightstand. A smile spread across her lips as she walked over to it and opened the drawer.

On top of her fantasy journal was a single condom and another red envelope. She picked up the condom and stifled a giggle when she saw that it was a special mint flavor.

She opened the envelope and read what would appear to be her last note.

Your hunt is almost over, my dear.

Return the mint and find your gift in the place that remains cold all year.

Brie stared down at her beloved journal, relieved to see that Sir had opened it. It meant that all was right with the world again. She walked back to Sir, proudly holding up the condom.

As with the other items, he placed it on the kitchen table and waited.

The last hint only stumped her for a second. She opened the freezer but did not find anything. She opened the refrigerator next, and squealed when she found a little black velvet bag.

Brie took it out and looked inside. She shivered as she pulled out a crystal-blue butt plug. She looked at him, suddenly worried. "This is cold, Sir."

His wicked smile gave her extra chills. "You may return it to the fridge, then kneel at my feet."

Brie put it back in the velvet bag and placed it on the shelf, shutting the door as goosebumps rose all over her skin. She went back to Sir and knelt as he'd commanded.

"Do you know what we have here?" he asked her, gesturing to the items on the table.

"Christmas fun?"

He chuckled. "Yes, that's one way to put it."

Sir picked up all the items and instructed her, "Go and freshen up, téa. Your Master is about to celebrate Christmas."

Brie literally ran to the bathroom, unable to rein in her excitement. She quickly washed up, brushed out her curls and spritzed Sir's favorite perfume on her wrists.

She returned to the living room to the sound of Christmas music filling the air. Sir was standing beside the Tantra chair, holding the velvet ribbon in his hands.

"Oh, Master…" she sighed as she glided over to him.

"Hands behind your back, téa."

He began the slow process of binding her arms with the soft ribbon, starting at her forearms and tying all the way down to her wrists. He ended it with a pretty bow she could barely see looking back over her shoulder.

"A gift wrapped for my enjoyment," he said, guiding her to lean her knees against the lower end of the Tantra chair, leaving her ass exposed and poised for play.

Sir disappeared for a moment, returning completely naked except for the red Santa hat she'd given him. He stood before her proudly, a smirk on his face. "Santa's come home from a long night of work and is ready to play."

She looked up at him, overcome by how sexy and adorable he looked. "How can I please you, Santa Claus?"

"You will find I am a demanding old man," he warned, picking up the large, decorative candy cane and examining it thoughtfully. "Who knew people decorated their yards with BDSM tools?" He smacked it against his palm. "They make the perfect toys." Sir patted the cane lightly against her butt.

She giggled. "Oh, if my dad only knew…he was so proud of his Candy Cane Lane when I was a kid."

"I bet he was."

Sir smacked her ass hard enough to make it sting, causing Brie to cry out.

He carefully moved the ends of the velvet bow out of his way and began softly stroking her with the cane, slowly building up the force behind each stroke. The plastic material of the decoration made it more flexible and stinging—a challenging tool to take.

"Would you like marks from Santa, little girl?"

"If it pleases you, Santa."

The next series of strokes took her breath away.

Sir stood back after he was done. "Beautiful. Now your naughty little ass is striped like a peppermint stick."

Brie looked back at him, her eyes watering. "Thank you, Santa."

One of his hands lovingly caressed the reddened area, while his other untied her from the velvet. Once she was free, he lifted her up and lay down on the tantra chair, commanding her to lie on him. The new position gave him free access to continue caressing her sore ass.

Sir reached over to the coffee table and picked up the two pretty tree decorations. "Santa had to look far and wide to find ornaments with the correct tension in the clip to provide a proper bite."

He played with her left nipple, pulling and rolling it between his fingers to make it ready. She stared down in fascination as he opened the clip and placed the sparkling snowflake on her erect nipple. Brie moaned with pleasure as the ache that the pressure caused traveled down to her groin.

Sir looked at her with a twinkle in his eyes as he applied the other ornament. She threw her head back and took in the wicked sensations his unique nipple clamps created as Sir massaged her breasts. Her pussy throbbed with pleasure from the attention, coating his cock with her juices.

He grabbed her hips and pushed her against his hard shaft. "I think it's time to treat Santa to a little show. Let me watch you ride Santa's pole."

Brie settled down on his cock, taking in the fullness of him. She loved that he watched her—the lust on his face as she moved up and down on his shaft was incredibly erotic. He continued to play with her breasts, tugging on the snowflakes for added stimulation.

Her heart skipped a beat when Sir threw his head back and let out a frustrated groan. He grasped her hips tightly and ordered her to stop. Brie didn't move a muscle as he struggled not to come.

Finally, he opened his eyes and stared at her. "Santa doesn't seem to have much restraint with you."

She moved slightly, taking him in a little deeper.

He immediately slapped her aching ass. "No moving, naughty girl."

Brie was thrilled by the power she had over him. Just another slight movement and her Master would be coming inside her against his will. The thought of that was intoxicating! But she was a good sub and didn't want to steal his power…at least not on Christmas Day. He was far too good a lover to play that kind of game.

"I believe a lesson is in order," he announced. Sir lifted her from him and stood up. He ordered her to lie stomach-first on the highest point of the chaise longue.

Brie stepped onto the curvature in the middle of the chair and lay against the soft leather, keeping her legs together. She loved how the chair supported the position. Her breasts rested on the highest curve, keeping them exposed for his play while giving him full access to her backside.

He picked up one of the strands of lights. "Time to restrain my naughty plaything." Sir started at her feet, wrapping them at the ankles, then brought the strand of lights under the chair to meticulously bind her wrists. He started with the second strand, but surprised her by binding the exact same areas.

Sir left her to turn out the overhead lights, then headed to the electrical outlet, stating, "Let there be light!"

When he plugged in the Christmas lights, he suggested that she look at the window. Brie saw in the reflection that she was bound in stripes of red and white, much like her striped ass.

"I love Santa," she purred.

The low temperature of the LED lights and the loose way he'd tied her made it a secure but comfortable binding. She was now officially a present tied up for Santa's kinky pleasure.

Sir unwrapped the large peppermint stick from the cellophane and asked, "If yard decorations make good canes, and ornaments are really nipple clamps, what do you think this is?"

She blushed when she answered hesitantly, "A dildo?"

He shook his head, tsking. "No, my dear. Candy should never be used for play in the nether regions. Unless, of course, you enjoy yeast infections." He lovingly caressed her mound. "One must always protect the chemistry of a woman's body."

Brie was deeply grateful that her Master was vigilant in his creative play.

Sir laid the Christmas towel next to her head and smiled wickedly. "Open."

Brie had to open wide, stretching her jaw muscles to take the circumference of the peppermint stick. She wrapped her lips around it, so the large stick wouldn't slip out. The mint had her instantly drooling onto her pretty towel.

Ball gags had always brought on a sense of humiliation for Brie. It wasn't just losing her voice during a scene, but losing the ability to control her body that made the experience unpleasant for her. However, Sir had made it sexy by using a tasty treat, along with his thoughtful placement of the towel. She embraced the loss of control and allowed her minty secretions to fall freely.

"Close your eyes, little girl," he growled softly in her ear.

Brie closed her eyes and listened for Sir. He moved around the chair, admiring the scene he'd created; his devoted sub tied in lights, gagged with a peppermint stick, while snowflake nipple clamps invited him to play.

Oh, how she loved her Master's creative mind.

She suddenly smelled the distinctive scent of pine before she felt the needles lightly brushing against her cheek, sending chills through her. He used the pine sprigs as a sensation tool, gently caressing her with the needles without scratching the skin.

"A light touch is needed," he murmured. He went for the sensitive areas, including her bare feet. Brie squirmed and wiggled, goosebumps rising on her skin. When his warm lips landed on the tingling areas he'd created, she instantly stilled.

"Good plaything."

Her pussy contracted with pleasure. Nothing was more erotic and satisfying than hearing words of praise spoken by her Master.

"You know, I've heard it's cold in Nebraska."

Sir left her again, then she heard the sound of the refrigerator opening. Brie shuddered. The idea of the cold crystal butt plug made her tremble with fear and expectation as he approached.

Sir smoothed warmed lubricant over her sphincter, adding to the temperature play about to happen. Brie moaned in response, dribbles of mint dropping from her lips.

"I want you to experience a true Nebraskan Christmas," he stated as he pushed the cold crystal against her tight ass.

Brie held her breath.

"Keep breathing," he reminded her, "and bear down for me."

She took in a deep breath before bearing down. Immediately, the ice-cold plug slipped inside her resistant hole. Her nipples contracted achingly from the sudden chill radiating from deep inside her, but her whimpers were muffled by the peppermint stick.

"That's it, naughty girl. Take that cold crystal for Santa," he murmured, removing the peppermint gag and wiping her lips with the towel.

Brie groaned with surprise when he kissed her. Sir tasted of rich chocolate, making a delicious combination of cocoa and mint. She lost herself in it, her body warmed by his passion as it was chilled by the toy.

After claiming her mouth, Sir stood before her so she could watch as he unrolled the mint condom over his rigid cock. "Are you ready to be fucked, plaything?"

Brie nodded eagerly. "I want to be fucked by your huge minty stick, Santa."

Sir chuckled as he positioned himself behind her. "Now we can both experience a cold Nebraskan winter." He eased his shaft into her tight pussy, made that much tighter by the cold crystal inside her ass.

His warm, thick shaft contrasted sharply with the cold butt plug, and they cried out in unison. "Fuuuuck! You're like ice," he growled lustfully, reaching around to play with her nipples.

He let her feel the tingling of his mint-covered cock before grabbing her hips and thrusting. The vigorous friction caused by his impassioned strokes began to counteract the cold between them.

Brie looked back at the reflection in the window, noticing that the sky was just starting to pinken with the approaching dawn as the song *It's Beginning to Look a Lot*

Like Christmas played in the background.

She had to stifle a giggle. There she was, tied in twinkly lights to a tantra chair, ornaments on her nipples, being pounded hard by her Master wearing a Santa hat. She knew she would never think of that song in the same way again.

Sir pulled out momentarily to remove the condom before diving back in. After several hearty thrusts, he became completely still, coming hard inside her. Brie cried out as his hot seed coated her chilled depths. In response, her pussy immediately clenched his shaft, milking him with her own powerful orgasm.

"Oh…my…Santa…" she panted.

Sir didn't move until the last pulse of her climax had ended. He pulled out slowly and rained kisses on her ass as he carefully removed the crystal. Then he unbound her. Once she was free, he lovingly unclamped a snowflake and sucked on her nipple to ease the pain of its release. He looked at her with a wicked grin as he removed the second one. Brie moaned with pleasure, enjoying the mixture of pleasure and pain the snowflakes caused.

Finally, Sir gathered her in his arms and cradled her against his chest, petting her hair gently in time with the music. Brie lay there, completely and beautifully spent, listening to the Christmas music and thinking that this had been the best Christmas ever—and then she saw it.

Mine

B rie spied a small box under the tiny Christmas tree. "Sir, is that another present?"

He looked in the direction of the Bonsai tree. "One has to wonder."

Brie grinned. "May I go and look?"

Sir released her from his embrace. "By all means, but first you have to kiss me."

She traced his lips with her finger before leaning in for the kiss. "And here I thought you didn't do Christmas." She got up and retrieved the thin box before returning to Sir's arms.

She slowly opened the lid of the red velvet box and put her hand to her lips when she saw what was inside. "Oh, Sir…"

He reached in and pulled out the strand of dark pearls. "They're Tahitian black pearls."

Brie took the necklace from him, looking at the iridescent sheen of the multicolored pearls. "I've never seen anything like them before. They're exquisite, Sir."

He took the necklace from her and looped the strand

once, putting it over her head and resting it between her breasts. "Knowing our history with pearls, I thought we might enjoy a fresh start."

She stroked the beads appreciatively. "This has to be the most wonderful Christmas gift I've ever gotten."

"That's not all, Brie."

She looked back in the box and saw a red envelope. "More?"

He nodded, a curious grin on his lips.

Brie picked it up and pulled out the card inside. She smiled as she looked at the card, but when she read the words, her bottom lip began to tremble.

You are MINE

Yet two things still separate us

A date

And a place

She opened the card and read:

You are cordially invited to the wedding of

Brianna Renee Bennett

and

Thane Lorenzo Davis

June 25

Brie stared at it, tears coming to her eyes. She whispered in disbelief, "We have a date."

"Yes."

"And the place?"

He caressed her cheek. "That, my beautiful sub, will remain my secret."

Brie would have protested, but she was far too thrilled knowing the date had finally been set for their wedding day—a dream come true.

She sighed happily. "June 25th…"

"Come hell or high water, we will be wed on that day," Sir assured her, laying Brie's head back against his chest. She closed her eyes, reveling in the sound of her Master's strong heartbeat.

In six months they would be man and wife—it was official now.

Merry Freakin' Christmas, Brie…

A Meal With Master

B rie stared into Sir's eyes as they lay together. He looked so serious… She sensed that he'd made an important decision but was still grappling with it. Their little 'holiday' from their problems hadn't fixed the issues they faced, but it had reconnected Brie to him on a soul level—and that was vital. They could survive anything as long as they remained connected to each other.

"Did I mention I loved spending Christmas morning with you, Sir?"

He smiled, brushing a strand of hair from her eye. "Yes, a number of times."

She turned and spooned against him, snuggling closer. "Spending time with you was the best present of all…"

Sir held her tight as they lay watching the sun slowly breach the horizon on the first day of the New Year, flooding the room with light. He gently nuzzled her ear with his lips before stating hoarsely, "I've decided to begin the process."

A dark current of fear coursed through Brie. It was

disconcerting when she knew it was a good thing that Sir was ready to take action. "With your mother?"

"Yes. I'm meeting with Thompson tomorrow. My mother has a mass of outstanding debts and I would like to know the full extent and nature of them."

Brie turned to face Sir, caressing his cheek lovingly. "This is a big step for you."

"I've given it an inordinate amount of thought. Initially, I believed it best to remember her as the woman I knew as a boy. However, I've come to the conclusion that I cannot let her die without understanding the woman she's become."

"That's courageous, Sir," she told him, but shuddered inwardly at the thought. "I worry that you may find out things that will upset or hurt you."

He gently traced his thumb over her downturned lips. "I'm the kind of person who prefers to know the truth rather than have things that are unpleasant kept from me. Unlike most people, ignorance is not my bliss."

She smiled, loving the ticklish feel of his touch. "Yes, I've learned that about you the hard way."

He chuckled, leaning over to kiss her on the lips. "But at least you learned."

Brie couldn't shake the ominous feeling associated with Sir and his mother and it confused her. She knew he needed to move forward, and the only way to do that was to wade through the mess his mother had made of her life. "I'll be with you every step of the way, Sir."

"I expect no less from my condor."

She settled back in his arms and sighed as she stared at the sun bathing the city with its golden light. It was impossible not to feel hope.

"Happy New Year, Sir…"

Brie stood in Mr. Holloway's office a month later, anxious to show him what she had filmed so far. She glanced down at the diamond ring on her finger and the pleasant butterflies started. She would be marrying Sir in less than five months…

Unfortunately, that left her little time to get all the filming complete for her second documentary. Wasting time going in a direction Mr. Holloway would not support was not an option for her, which was why she'd requested the special meeting.

Brie noticed that he watched Headmaster Coen's entire spanking scene while wearing a slight smirk on his face. Afterwards he turned to Brie, shaking his head. "This one is flirting with an XXX rating, Miss Bennett. I counted four orgasms, possibly five."

"While I know it's obvious to you and me, I doubt the audience will pick up on it. I find most people are ignorant of the orgasms happening around them."

"It *is* uniquely provocative, but I want you to edit portions of it, possibly film a few extra shots if you can't make it less obvious. I'm interested in keeping the segment, but we don't want your work confused with a pornographic film."

Brie felt the heat rise to her cheeks. "I'll work on the edits and talk to Headmaster Coen if needed."

Next she showed him her flogging scene with Marquis.

Mr. Holloway studied it with great interest, giving Brie reason to believe he'd enjoyed the scene. However, he stunned her when he announced afterwards, "This will *not* be included in your film."

"Bu—"

"End of discussion."

Brie hated the thought of telling Marquis Gray that his scene had been cut. It was a beautiful encounter, and was significant to her on a personal level. The scene was every bit as provocative and artful as the spanking scene, and Brie felt the urge to defend it. Yet when she studied the producer's face, his expression let her know there would be no budging on this point.

"Can I have an explanation, please?"

Instead of answering her, Mr. Holloway stated, "You mentioned a meeting with the head trainer of the Dominant course at the Center. How did that go?"

Brie saw the challenge in his eye, daring her to ask again about Marquis' scene. She reluctantly accepted the change of subject, not wanting to lose her documentary over it, although she feared it would be a disappointment to Marquis Gray, a Dom she highly respected.

"Master Nosh was busy, but I was told he might be willing to do an interview with me."

"I leave it up to you whether you want to pursue that further. I'm interested in what he has to say, but am unsure if it will have any relevance to your film. Where are you headed next?"

"I plan to visit Mr. Wallace and Miss Wilson at the

Sanctuary in Montana. I sent a wire, since I am unable to contact them by phone, and received confirmation a few days ago that I would be welcome to join the commune for a two-week stay."

"Now *that* I am interested in. Send me the raw footage when you're done."

Brie was unsure why he was so fascinated with the commune, but thought it might have something to do with Mary. He'd shown an interest in her story when Brie was filming her first documentary. At the time, she'd assumed it was for purely professional reasons. Now she wasn't so sure…

"Certainly. I'll send it to you first thing, Mr. Holloway. As for the rest, I plan to have all the shooting done and the basic editing complete before June."

"Before the wedding, then? A wise choice, Miss Bennett. I have no patience for people's personal lives interfering with business."

"It won't, Mr. Holloway. I assure you. Sir Davis and I are agreed that the filming comes first."

"Fine, then you may see yourself out."

She stood up and nodded respectfully to him before walking towards the door.

"Don't forget, Miss Bennett, I want that footage as soon as possible."

Brie smiled to herself. He really must have a thing for Mary. Too bad the girl was already taken…

Since Sir was meeting with his lawyer in the same area of town, they met for lunch afterwards. She felt that familiar flush as she spied him sitting at a corner table. He looked so confident and handsome sitting there alone. It humbled Brie knowing that Sir was waiting for her, and the smile on his face when he spotted her across the room absolutely melted her heart.

"Please sit," he said, guiding her to the chair beside him. "I've already ordered an appetizer."

While Brie munched on the fresh fruit and cheeses he'd ordered, she explained how she'd fared in her meeting with Mr. Holloway. Underneath the table, Sir hiked up her skirt so he could stroke her smooth thigh.

"It sounds as if he's interested in your latest endeavor."

Brie smiled, unwilling to share her suspicions concerning Mr. Holloway's true motivations. Sir hated gossips. Unless she had indisputable evidence, it was best to say nothing. "Yes, he continues to be interested in the documentary, but I'm really disappointed I'm losing the flogging scene."

"That is a shame, Brie," he replied, slipping his hand between her legs. "I had hoped your father would see it and come to understand his daughter better."

She opened her legs to him, allowing her Master greater access.

"Me too, Sir. It was a powerful scene on many levels." Brie stopped eating, distracted by the electricity caused by his sensual touch.

"Have another slice of apple," Sir commanded gently as he swirled his finger over her clit.

She suppressed the squeak that burst forth as she took a slice and bit into it. Sir was so wickedly bad.

The waiter came up and smiled at Brie. "Miss, have you decided on a plate?"

She looked at Sir, the heat rising to her cheeks as he increased the delightful pressure on her clit. "I...umm..."

"We'll share a plate of your cock stuffed with brie."

"Do you mean our stuffed chicken breast, sir?"

"Exactly," Sir replied with a smirk.

"A fine choice," the waiter complimented, turning to Brie and giving her a wink before leaving.

"He seems to be smitten with you, my dear," Sir growled, slowly sinking his finger into her. Brie held her breath and remained still, every fiber of her being concentrated on the pressure of his finger. "Eat," he reminded her.

She lifted the slice of apple to her lips, her gaze locked on to Sir's. In a crowded restaurant, in the middle of the day, he was having his way with her. It was insanely sexy.

When the waiter returned with their dish, Sir pulled his finger from her and sucked it in front of the man. "I do enjoy the taste of Brie in the afternoon."

"Certainly, sir." The waiter placed the dish in front of them, adding, "The creamy texture of a good brie enhances the culinary experience."

Brie giggled, looking at Sir as she quipped, "So I've been told."

"If you require anything else, miss, please don't hesitate to ask."

She felt her Master's hand return between her legs and let out a satisfied sigh. "Thank you, but I have everything I need."

"Very well," the waiter answered, obviously discouraged by her dismissive tone.

After he left, Sir leaned over and whispered in her ear, "I do believe you just broke his young heart."

The heat in Brie's cheeks increased as Sir resumed his forbidden caress. "Cut off a piece of that breast and feed it to me, téa."

She picked up the fork and knife with trembling hands, and attempted to slice through the bird while her pussy caught fire with need. She bit her lip in concentration as she brought the piece of succulent meat oozing with brie to his lips.

"Look into my eyes," he said before taking the bite.

Brie gazed into them, a chill settling on her as her body primed for release.

He nodded slightly, giving her permission…

With a tiny squeak, she gave in to the fire. Her whole body shook as a wave of intense pleasure washed over her.

Sir swallowed his bite and smiled. "Good girl…"

He sucked his finger again, relishing her taste before taking the fork and knife from her. "Let me cut you a piece now."

Their meal was sensual and private, even though they were in the midst of a crowd. Sir had that unique and beautiful effect on her. She was sad when the check was paid and they were forced to go their separate ways.

"I want you to set up your travel arrangements for the Montana trip when you get home. Unfortunately, I will not be able to join you."

"Traveling is much more pleasant when you're with me," Brie said, silently pleading he would change his mind.

"However, it's not a reality for us. As a film director, you will often find yourself traveling alone. The secret lies in how we structure our time apart."

Brie nodded, sighing with resignation.

"You must keep a tight schedule if we are to wed this June," he reminded her, taking Brie's hand and kissing the ring on her finger.

"Well, when you put it that way, Sir… I'll be sure to make those arrangements as soon as I get home."

"That's better. We'll discuss the logistics of our separation tonight."

As she walked to her car once they'd parted ways, Brie fought off the sense of sadness that washed over her. Any time apart was hard on her, but she was determined to succeed with this second film. The world would be a better place because of her sacrifice and dedication; she had to trust and believe in that.

Big Sky Country

Although she faithfully wrote to Tono Nosaka every week, it was rare for him to respond. She impatiently opened his letter, anxious to learn how Tono was faring in Japan.

Dear Brie,

It pleases me to hear your meeting with Mr. Holloway went well and that you've been given the green light to continue filming. Naturally, if we should meet again, I would be honored to film a session of Kinbaku for you, although the opportunity seems highly unlikely at this point.

Despite my best efforts, my mother has become more discontented with time. To preserve my sanity, I took your recommendation to continue working on my modern take on Kinbaku. Chikako and I have made steady progress. It's brought me much-needed peace and I thank you for being forthright in your suggestion.

Against my mother's wishes, I have passed on my father's studio to a well-respected bakushi, a man worthy of continuing my father's legacy. I have neither the time nor the interest to run it. If I am completely honest, I did not want the responsibility, knowing it would cement my fate here in Japan. Although I fully accept my duty, I still hope to return to America someday. It is a purely selfish desire, but to deny it would be foolish.

I have not said anything until now, but I find it touching that you wear my orchid whenever you film. As you know, I admire your talent and am proud to be a part of the process—even if only in spirit. Please continue to send your letters. They are something I have come to look forward to each week.

Enjoy your time at the commune. I'm certain it will be a fascinating experience. I trust Mr. Wallace will behave himself while you're there. I would be remiss if I did not admit my concern. However, I know your Master is invested in your wellbeing and would not put you in harm's way.

In all things, I wish you continued growth and peace. Give my best to Sir Davis.

Respectfully,
Ren Nosaka

Brie sighed as she placed Tono's letter inside the silk satchel, along with the others he'd sent. She saw a vision of his warm, chocolate-brown eyes and smiled.

"I'm praying you return home, Tono."

To her delight, Sir had insisted on taking her to the airport despite the earliness of her flight. He reached out as he drove, tenderly caressing her cheek. "Don't fret. It is only a temporary separation."

"I know, Sir, but I dislike leaving you, especially now because of what's happened to your mother."

"Although I appreciate your concern, I'll be fine."

"But if you need me to return for any reason, do you promise to contact me?" she pleaded. "It's going to be hard enough not talking to you while I'm at the commune, but I won't be able to focus on this assignment unless I'm certain you will let me know if things get worse."

"If her condition changes, I will send for you," he assured her.

"Not having daily contact with you is going to kill me, Sir."

"However, we must abide by the rules of the commune," he reminded her. "It's not as if we haven't been down this road before, when you were under Nosaka's care, and we have our protocols set. It will not be as difficult as you think."

Brie wiggled in her seat, feeling the comforting presence of her jewelry as it pressed against her clit. Wearing the intimate jewelry would definitely help to comfort her when she found herself longing for him.

"Keep your eye on the prize, Brie. I expect you to pursue it with dogged vigilance."

"I will, Sir," she said, smiling sadly, "but my heart will be pining away for you."

"As long as it doesn't affect the quality of your work," he chided teasingly.

"I promise to come back with footage that will amaze and astound you."

Sir chuckled as he parked the Lotus. "Mr. Holloway is the only one you need to impress, babygirl."

Before he left her at the airport, Sir kissed her deeply, prolonging the kiss so that all her attention was focused on him and nothing else. When he finally broke the contact, he smiled down at her.

Brie sighed. "Your kisses are like magic for my soul."

He grazed her lips with his fingertips. "I'm in agreement with you."

Sir walked away, moving through the airport with a confident stride that caught the attention of those around him. She allowed herself a moment to mourn their separation before turning away and walking in the opposite direction with an equally confident stride. She was a film director. All her energy needed to be centered on that for the next two weeks. There was no time for sentimentality.

Brie was surprised how far out the commune was from Whitefish, Montana. Truly, no one would stumble upon the place by accident. She knew she'd finally made it to her destination when she saw the gate, but there was no signage other than a warning posted on the gate that stated, *Trespassers will be shot*.

She was unsure whether it was meant as a humorous warning or a serious threat.

Brie saw there was a rusty intercom, and rolled down the car window to press the red button on the keypad. It crackled to life and a male voice with a distinctive drawl said, "State your name and order of business."

"Hello, I'm Brianna Bennett. Master Gannon is expecting me."

The intercom went dead. After several agonizing moments, it crackled again. "You may enter."

The gate creaked and complained as it slowly swung open. The secluded environment, the warning sign, the old equipment along with the thickly wooded area made Brie think of the movie *Deliverance*. She suddenly wondered if she should be concerned for her safety as she drove through the rusty gate.

As Brie drove down the winding dirt road, images of rustic cabins, rocking chairs and men with overgrown beards crowded her mind. When she rounded the last bend, the wooded area opened up and revealed a delightful surprise.

The commune was not a rundown cabin community at all. Oh, no…this establishment looked like a first-class resort. The main building was covered in scenic windows, multiple balconies and an elaborate stone patio that surrounded the entire structure.

When she saw two men approaching her on the

road, she slowed the car to a stop and unrolled her window again. "Is either of you Master Gannon?"

"No, I am one of the Gatekeepers. Hand over your keys and your cell phone. Both will be returned to you when it's time for you to leave."

Brie was startled by the demand, but got out of the rental car, grabbing her suitcase and camera equipment before handing over her keys.

"Rajah will help with your luggage."

Rajah looked nothing like the mountain man she'd expected to see. He was tall and tan, with long dark hair and mischievous green eyes. Without asking permission, he grabbed her luggage and all her equipment before starting towards the building.

The Gatekeeper noticed the concern on Brie's face and assured her, "Rajah will take care of your belongings."

"But my camera equip—"

"Gannon is waiting for you, Miss Bennett."

Brie understood that to mean she was wasting Master Gannon's time. The last thing she wanted was to make a poor impression on the leader of the commune. It had been highly unusual to be invited as a guest, so she hastened towards the building.

An older man who looked to be in his sixties stood waiting for her on the steps. He had the unusual combination of one brown and one blue eye, which instantly drew her attention. She had to force herself not to stare in order not to appear rude. Brie held out her hand and was relieved when he shook it cordially.

"Thank you for letting me visit your commune, Master Gannon."

"That's simply Gannon to you."

"Yes, Gannon," she replied, immediately correcting herself.

A large black cat came up to him and rubbed against his legs. Master Gannon smiled as he picked it up. "So, Miss Bennett, what do you think of my utopia?"

She glanced up at the impressive building before her. "The Sanctuary is nothing like I imagined."

"This has been my lifelong vision," he stated proudly.

"You have an exquisite imagination, sir."

"I knew it would become reality, but I had to be patient and invite the right people to share in my dream. Although I've agreed to let you join us for several weeks, you are not allowed to shoot footage of any of the buildings on the estate. I want to promote the idea that we live a simple life to the outside world."

"What am I allowed to film, then?"

"Any outdoor activities. You may also interview interested members. However, the lush accommodations, as well as the exact location, must remain secret. I do not want our way of life disrupted by the curious and unvetted."

"Can I ask why you've agreed to let me film here if you want to keep your privacy?"

"I hope my vision will inspire others like it. America has been bound by laws created by prudish misfits. It is time to open our minds and bodies to something greater."

"It seems you're talking about more than just sexual

freedom."

He cocked his head and smiled as he petted the cat. "You're perceptive, Miss Bennett. Before I subject you to a political lecture, I suggest you seek out your friends. I believe they are waiting for you in the garden."

Brie turned in the direction he'd pointed to and spied Faelan standing next to a large fountain. She excused herself, giving the cat a scratch under its chin before leaving the Master.

Todd Wallace looked leaner than she remembered, and she noticed a wildness in his eyes that she hadn't seen before. It made the young Dom even more striking, but it unsettled her on a gut level she couldn't understand. There was nothing sexual about his feral look.

Mary, on the other hand, looked totally relaxed and in her element. Brie had never seen her friend exude such easy confidence. Unlike the Blonde Nemesis of her training days, Mary seemed comfortable and *very* content.

"Well, look what the cat dragged in…"

"Hey, bitch," Brie answered good-naturedly. "Too good to contact me just to let me know you're okay? I assume you're free to leave the commune to connect with friends and family on occasion."

Mary looked around, gesturing to several shirtless men in cowboy hats walking past, and shrugged. "If given the choice, I would pick staying here and playing with them every time. In fact…I have."

Brie glanced at Faelan, curious whether he was jealous hearing Mary speak like that. She was surprised to see Todd's expression change as he stared at Mary. It was a protective but loving look, and made Brie reconsider her initial unease about him. Maybe this commune *was* a healthy environment for them both.

"Why did I even bother to come?" Brie teased.

"I don't know. It's not like I asked you to visit."

Faelan put his arm around Mary. "Now, now…" He looked at Brie with those mesmerizing blue eyes and said, "Don't let her bitterness fool you. She's been anxious for your arrival."

Mary elbowed him in the gut. "Shut the fuck up, Faelan."

He raised his eyebrow. "What did we say about the word 'fuck'?"

She let out an irritated sigh. "We only use it as a verb."

"That's right," he replied smoothly. "Drop and give me twenty."

Mary put her hands on her hips. "Don't do this. Not in front of Stinky Cheese."

"We agreed," he answered her.

Mary huffed as she reluctantly got down on the ground and began counting out twenty pushups. Brie had to cover her mouth to keep from laughing seeing Mary submit so readily to Faelan.

"Who the hell is this girl, and what did you do with Mary?" Brie demanded.

Faelan smiled charmingly. "Same girl, different attitude."

Mary continued with her pushups without adding her own snarky remark, but in her attempt to hurry, her pushups became shallow. Faelan put his foot on Mary's back, forcing her to lie still on the ground.

"Try that again. Nose to the dirt—don't half-ass it."

To Brie's surprise, Mary didn't argue as she started counting from one again.

Brie looked wide-eyed at Faelan, her mouth agape in sheer disbelief.

Mary looked up. "Hey, stop gawking at my man."

"But I've never seen you so…domesticated. This place is starting to remind me a little of the *Stepford Wives*."

Mary hesitated for a second, but Faelan reminded her, "Unless you want to start over, I suggest you continue."

Mary completed her set and got back up, wiping her hands on her skirt. Instead of verbally flaying Brie, she turned to Faelan. "I…apologize, Faelan."

"Kiss me," he ordered.

Mary leaned in to him and they kissed for several long, drawn-out minutes. Normally, Brie would have been irritated being forced to watch Blonde Nemesis play tonsil-hockey for such a long time, but it warmed her heart to see the two so hot for each other.

When Faelan pulled away, he brushed his finger over her lips. "Pedestrian curses only taint this beautiful mouth."

A smile tugged on Mary's lips.

"It appears commune life agrees with you, Mary Quiet Contrary," Brie complimented.

She nodded in agreement, not taking her eyes off Faelan. "You have no idea."

"So show me around the place. I want to discover what makes it such a transformative setting."

"Yes, why don't you take Brie for a tour of the grounds?" Faelan suggested. He grabbed Mary's chin possessively and kissed her again before letting go.

Mary shuddered in reaction to his impassioned kiss. "Fine, I will."

Faelan turned his attention back to Brie. "I look forward to hearing what you think of the Sanctuary once you've seen all it has to offer."

The Sanctuary

Mary pointed towards the main lodge building. "That's where we all live and do most of our play, but let me show you the estate first."

"You know," Brie said as they walked, "when you told me you were living at a commune, I had images of log cabins and old hippies running around. I wasn't prepared for it to be a high-class resort."

Mary scoffed. "Just because we're self-sufficient doesn't mean we have to live deprived lives."

"So how do you guys support a place like this? Were you required to invest your own money to join?"

"Hell, no. Master Gannon built it before the stock market crashed in 2001. He used all his investments to build the entire estate. Since our community lives off the grid, each of us is required to help maintain the grounds and make enough to meet the needs of all of the members."

Brie was impressed. "So how does one become a member?"

"Master Gannon hand-selects the people he wants to

populate it. The vetting process is quite lengthy. Not only does the couple have to be experienced kinksters, they have to possess additional skills that can be utilized by the community. We're all expected to volunteer our time and expertise in order to keep the commune running efficiently."

"So you're required to work every day solely to support the commune without getting paid?"

"Our payment is getting to live here."

"So what specific skills did you and Todd bring to the community?"

"The commune recently lost their pharmacist, so I was a shoe-in when the man left to start a family. As for Faelan, he had his physical brawn and multiple BDSM skills to bring to the table."

Mary pointed to a huge, wooden barn. "The livestock and horses are kept there. Not only do we breed and train horses, but every morsel of meat we consume is born, raised and butchered on this property."

She pointed out a huge vegetable garden and orchard, with rolling wheat fields behind it. "Every vegetable, grain and fruit consumed comes from our own garden. It's empowering to be responsible for every aspect of our lives."

Brie looked at the snow-covered peaks in the distance. "How does the community support itself through the winter?"

"Nothing is cooked out of season, unless we've canned or preserved it." Mary pointed to another large structure west of the barn. "We also make BDSM furniture to sell."

"So you're kind of like the Amish."

Mary snorted. "Sure...but with awesome sex and modern conveniences thrown in."

Brie giggled, catching the attention of several males as they walked by. She noticed they nodded to Mary but completely ignored her. She found it curious but wasn't necessarily surprised. Having hung out with Mary in the past, she was used to Mary's power of attraction.

*Fucking blondes...*she thought, shaking her head in amusement.

"Out in the woods we have different areas designed for kinky play."

Brie looked at her oddly. "But you don't seem the nature type to me."

"Oh, I've screamed in the woods multiple times. But you're right, I prefer to stay indoors. You'll understand why when I show you..." Mary led Brie through the large doors of the main building.

The entrance opened up into a giant room with vaulted ceilings, an impressive fireplace made of river rock and a ridiculously long sectional couch in the center. Various play furniture lined the walls, including several styles of tantra chairs—one of which was currently in use.

"Oh, Mary! This is a kinkster's dream palace," Brie whispered.

"Yes, it is."

Mary smiled at the couple fucking on the chair as she led Brie to the other side of the spacious room.

It was strange. Mary was acting so... pleasant and normal. It was hard to believe she was the same person

Brie had trained with at the Center.

"And downstairs we have the bedrooms," Mary informed her, pointing to a set of stairs.

"Can I see yours?" Brie asked, curious what they looked like after seeing the impressive main room.

Mary shrugged. "They're nothing special, Brie. We just sleep there, so they're small and unadorned. Master Gannon wants us interacting as a group during the day." To Brie's delight, Mary changed direction and led her down the long flight of stairs, walking past numerous doors of various colors in the narrow hallway.

Mary abruptly stopped and turned, opening a blue one. "This is Faelan's and my room."

Brie walked inside and whistled. There was only enough space for the king-sized bed, a closet and a private toilet. Brie's luggage had been piled in the corner, taking up the remaining space. The only design element of any interest was the impressive mirror mounted on the ceiling.

"Wow, girl. You weren't kidding about these rooms being small. It's reminiscent of a college dorm."

"Yes, but the beds are designed for fucking."

Brie jumped on the large bed and fell backwards, testing it out by rolling and gyrating on it.

"What the hell, Brie?"

"Just testing it out for myself. I have to agree, the bed seems sturdy enough for Todd's brand of spirited play."

Mary gave her a knowing smile. "Yeah, but the bed's barely strong enough for the two of us." Then she huffed in irritation. "But unfortunately for me, I'm stuck housing you for the next two weeks."

"What? All three of us here?" Brie asked, suddenly concerned.

"No, you twit. Faelan's been invited to join another couple. Damn, I wish it were me, but no...I get stuck sleeping with you."

Brie jumped off the bed, feeling relieved. "Hey, you'd better not get any ideas. I'm not into women, especially not bitchy blondes."

"Hah! Like you would ever be good enough for me."

As they walked back down the hallway, Brie asked, "Does it bother you that Todd will be with others at night?"

Mary stopped and stared at her as if she were a simpleton. "Are you kidding me? This is a commune—we share everything. Besides, you see the way Faelan looks at me. He may fuck the other girls here, but that boy's heart is all mine."

Brie nudged her. "I did notice that, and it seems to go both ways."

Mary gave her an irritated look. "I'm not you. God, why do you always have to assume I'm as lovesick and stupid as you are?" She tromped up the stairs, forcing Brie to run to catch up. The bitch might have changed in many ways, but she was still just as impossible.

Mary nonchalantly pointed out the large dining room. It was truly impressive, with a single, incredibly long table and all the numerous chairs that surrounded it. "Master Gannon insists we eat dinner together every night, no exceptions. He says mealtime is when familial connections are made and cemented."

She opened two swinging doors just right of the table. "And here is the kitchen. Everyone in the commune is required to cook. Tonight happens to be my night, but I warned them not to let you anywhere near the kitchen."

"Shows how much you know," Brie stated smugly. "I can cook killer dishes these days."

Mary snorted. "Killer is right."

"They're delicious. Even Sir approves. Boa took me under his wing and taught me."

"You mean under his cock?"

Brie giggled at the reference to the sub's colossal shaft. "Bet you didn't know Boa is a patient teacher. Far more patient than Marquis Gray."

"Yeah, I'll never forget the look on Marquis' face when you kept presenting him with your crappy omelets."

"Yours weren't any better."

"Hell yes, they were. I beat you out of the kitchen that day, didn't I?"

Brie rolled her eyes. "Well, now I can cook several authentic Italian dishes, but because of what you just said I'm not going to cook them for you—ever."

"Thank God," Mary said with sarcastic enthusiasm.

"I'm shocked they let *you* in the kitchen."

"I'm perfectly capable of prepping, and…I provide 'release' for the chefs."

"Ah, your true worth revealed."

Mary grabbed a large knife and waved it teasingly at Brie. "Unlike you, I have many talents."

Brie held up her arms in mock surrender. "Look, I'm

not into knife play, but if you insist…"

Mary dropped the knife back onto the counter just as a fine-looking cowboy strutted into the kitchen. He took one look at Mary from under his wide-brimmed hat and tsked disapprovingly. "You're to treat the instruments of this kitchen with the respect they deserve."

Mary immediately picked up the knife and carefully slid it into the wooden block, looking sheepishly at him. Brie loved it. For all her bravado, Mary was still as much of a goof as she was. It was comforting to know.

"Yes, let me show you the equipment upstairs now, Miss Bennett," she said in an official tone, leading Brie out of the kitchen under the intense stare of the sexy cowboy. "It's my favorite place to play because of the view and exposure."

They climbed a long spiral staircase that led up to a row of separate play rooms. The first had a medical theme, complete with examining table, a wall of medical equipment, and scrubs. Brie shuddered and quickly made her way to the next room. Her heart skipped a beat when she saw the variety of floggers and the binding post. It appeared each room had its own theme with corresponding instruments and furniture to match, very similar to The Haven.

"Nice…" Brie complimented.

Mary smiled mischievously as she led Brie into the third room. Brie stopped short when she saw the wall of knives, needles and piercing equipment.

"Here we can enjoy blood play all we want. No restrictions other than safety."

Brie slowly backed out of the room. "I think I'll

pass."

"You're such a baby."

"And proud of it," Brie stated.

"But this is the best part," Mary told her, dragging her out onto the balcony.

Brie caught her breath. The view overlooking the lake was magnificent, absolutely stunning. The beauty of the snowy peaks surrounding them was reflected in the still water. "Oh, wow…"

"There are four balconies up here, each facing in a different direction," Mary informed her.

Brie did not miss all the binding equipment stored in the glass case next to her. Before she could ask about it, the cowboy from the kitchen appeared beside Mary.

"Remove your panties, go to the railing and kneel facing me."

Mary instantly obeyed, as if it were Faelan who'd commanded her. After removing her thong, she knelt with her legs spread apart in an inviting manner, the shortness of her skirt exposing her blonde pussy to him.

The Dom grabbed nylon rope from the case and took her wrists, binding them together before securing them to the railing so she was immobilized.

"Open," he commanded, tilting his hat back so he could observe her.

Mary obediently opened her crimson lips, glancing up at the man with a sexy look of fear and anticipation— the perfect submissive.

He unzipped his pants and pulled his erect cock from his jeans, easing it into her mouth. "Deep-throat it, darlin'."

Brie remembered Mary's skill at sucking cock, and was impressed yet again as she watched her friend take the length of the man's shaft down her throat. He fisted her long blonde hair and thrust deeper, then began pumping vigorously as if he were fucking her pussy. Mary took it with grace, never losing eye contact as he thrust into her mouth. It was actually beautiful to watch, but it was his grunts of satisfaction that deeply affected Brie.

She felt a trickle of excitement travel past her clit jewelry and down her leg. It was definitely going to be hard living in the commune for the next few weeks, knowing she would be a witness to all kinds of kinky fun with no outlet for release. Sir had specifically ordered her not to masturbate while they were apart.

Damn...

The cowboy pulled out and caressed Mary's cheek. "I could fuck your lips all day, darlin'."

She smiled up at him. "I would be honored to service you."

He shook his head. "Unfortunately, there's a filly that needs breaking. I'll have to be satisfied with this for now." He rubbed the tip of his cock over her lips before taking her mouth again. This time he grabbed Mary's head with both hands and pumped forcefully into her, crying out when his orgasm finally hit.

Brie swallowed hard, looking out over the lake as she tried to concentrate on the beauty of the scenery rather than her own sexual need.

Missing you, Sir.

After he'd finished, the cowboy untied Mary and

helped her to her feet. He tipped his hat to her. "Tomorrow, same time and place."

Mary nodded demurely.

The Dom kissed her well-used lips, all smeared with red lipstick, before leaving the girls alone on the balcony.

"So that's a common occurrence?" Brie whispered.

Mary wiped her mouth with her forearm, a smirk on her lips. "Any Dom can take you at any time. It makes daily life on the commune most enjoyable for a sub."

"Are you allowed to say no?"

"Naturally, but why the hell would I?" Mary pointed to a charming bridge in the distance. "I need to clean up. Why don't I meet you down there?"

"Sure," Brie answered. She admired the view from the other three balconies before following a second spiral staircase down and heading outside. The blueness of the Montana sky reminded her of Colorado and made her think of Lea.

"Girlfriend, I think you would go nuts here," Brie said out loud, laughing to herself.

She followed the dirt path to a footbridge that crossed over a stream, which fed into the mountain lake. She soaked in the sounds of rushing water as jays chirped above her in the pine trees. It was truly a relaxing environment...

"Strip and present yourself to me."

Kinky Fun

B rie opened her eyes and turned slowly to face the Dom who had commanded her. She was shocked to see Faelan staring at her lustfully. Although she knew such practices were common here, she'd never expected anyone to demand that of her as a guest of the commune—least of all Faelan.

She didn't make a move.

"Are you refusing a direct command?"

Although she was still aroused from Mary's recent encounter and her body naturally responded to his animal magnetism, she wasn't about to submit to him.

Brie held her head high and answered with a defiant, "Yes."

Faelan's demeanor completely changed. She'd expected anger; instead he started laughing. "Mary insisted I have a little fun with you, and I couldn't resist when I saw you here alone." He shook his head. "That look on your face was comical." He continued to laugh at her expense as he leaned against the handrail beside her.

"Very funny," she growled, not enjoying being the

butt of Mary and Faelan's joke.

"Just so we're clear, Brie, I would have refused you if you had stripped. In this community you're considered untouchable until you've gone through Initiation. You're basically invisible to all the Doms here."

So that explains why I've been treated like a ghost.

Brie was used to Doms sizing her up before checking her neck to see if she was wearing a collar, but the Doms here had made her feel as if she didn't exist. It'd reminded her a bit of her tobacco shop days—before Sir had found her and changed everything.

"Just so *we're* clear," she told Faelan, wanting to put him in his place, "I never considered stripping for you."

"Oh, I saw that moment of hesitation when you considered it."

"Your arrogance never ceases to amaze me."

"Don't worry, I won't tell."

"There's nothing to tell!"

He chuckled again. "It's good to see you again, blossom. Mary's missed you, even if she refuses to admit it."

Brie should have protested the use of his pet name for her, but the way he said it was casual, like a nickname between old friends. It felt comfortable.

"Somehow I doubt she missed me."

"You have more influence on her than you know."

"She seems quite happy here. Happier than I thought she was capable of, truthfully."

"Yes, I think she gains strength from being here at the commune." Brie noticed a brief look of pain flit across his face and wondered at the cause of it. Before she could ask, Mary strolled up.

Faelan wrapped his arms around Mary and kissed the top of her head. "I heard Marcus was looking for you."

She smiled. "Oh…he found me."

"Good. I like having the sub everyone else wants to enjoy."

"I like being that sub," she replied conceitedly.

"I bet you do," he growled, nipping Mary's shoulder.

Brie was pleased to see how relaxed and attentive the two were towards each other. It would have been obnoxious if it hadn't been so genuine. Despite the challenges of having an open relationship, they seemed to be flourishing in this environment.

"So on a scale of one to ten, how would you rate commune life?" she asked Mary.

Mary snuggled against Faelan. "If you'd told me life could be like this, I would have socked you in the jaw for being a f—" she looked warily at Faelan and corrected herself, "…a liar."

He fisted Mary's hair. Her old habit of flinching caused her to cower momentarily in fear, but she soon relaxed when he grabbed her chin and kissed her deeply. "Yeah, I've got no complaints about this place," he said gruffly.

"So what about you, Brie?" Mary asked. "How's the vanilla world treating you these days?"

Brie couldn't hold in her excitement when she told Mary, "Sir and I are getting married in June!"

"Oh God, can you get any more vanilla than that?" Mary complained, rolling her eyes.

Brie laughed. "You can dis me all you want, bitch, but I'm one happy little sub." She looked at her ring, the diamond sparkling with an allure similar to Sir's eyes.

"Do what makes you happy, blossom," Faelan replied, sounding sincere.

"Thanks. I am happy, but I'll be even happier once I get this second documentary finished."

"Your time isn't going to be all work here, is it?" Mary complained. "I have a few things I want to share with you that are much too scandalous to make it into your vanilla BDSM documentary."

Brie ignored her teasing. "Sure. I'm hoping to spend time alone with you too."

Mary laughed. "Oh, Brie, you really are a twit."

Before Brie could take offense, Faelan spoke up. "Mary is in serious need of some girl-time. She hates to admit it, but you keep her grounded."

Now it was Mary's turn to be offended. "Grounded? What the f—" She regained her composure and asked, "What do you mean by that, Faelan?"

He patted her on the shoulder. "And on that note, I'll bid you *adieu*." He chuckled to himself as he walked towards the barn.

Mary stared at Brie with her lips pursed. "I don't need grounding, bitch."

"I wouldn't give it to you even if you asked."

Blonde Nemesis broke out in laughter. "Damn, Brie. I forgot you were funny. Always lump you in with Lea and her pathetic attempts at humor."

They sat on some boulders beside the stream to talk. "Admit it, Mary, there are times you laugh at Lea's silly jokes."

"No…I laugh *at* her, not with her."

"Someday I will get you to confess your love for Lea *and* her lame jokes." Seeing she wasn't going to convince Mary of that anytime soon, Brie asked, "So you mentioned wanting to share something with me?"

Mary's eyes lit up. "Oh, yes! I have three guys interested in trying it with me and I want you to film the event. But you can't use it for your damn documentary—this is for my private use only!"

"What exactly do you want me to film?"

She grinned, looking like a naughty schoolgirl. "I want to do a foursome."

"What's the big deal?" Brie was less than impressed.

"I want to take all three cocks at the same time."

Brie was imagining a DP with a little oral action. "So?"

Mary leaned in close. "I want to take two cocks in my pussy and one up my ass."

Brie looked at her in disbelief. "Oh, now that *is* different."

"Yeah…" Mary said with a self-satisfied smile.

"Is Todd—"

Mary waved off the question before she'd even asked. "He doesn't care to scene with other Doms."

Brie tried to wrap her mind around the idea. "How can your body take it? I mean, is your twat so huge you can handle two shafts?"

"Are you just trying to bait me so I beat the shit out of you?"

Keeping her smile to herself, Brie answered, "No, I'm honestly curious."

"I don't have a giant cunt, bitch. It's going to be a

real challenge for me, but that's why I like the idea."

"That's all kinds of unnatural stretching."

Mary's eyes took on a dreamy look. "Being rammed by three cocks at once… Fuck, does it get any hotter than that?"

Brie shook her head. "I can't even imagine it, but I guess I won't have to."

"So you're willing to film it?"

"Sure, why not? As long as Todd's cool with it."

"Fuck, he's open to me trying anything."

"Hmm… I notice your language slips when he's not around. Should I enlighten him?"

Mary tilted her chin up and sneered. "I only clean up my language for him. You, on the other hand, don't matter to me."

"It's no wonder you don't have any girlfriends here, based on the way you treat me."

"I like putting you in your place—someone needs to," Mary huffed.

"I feel the same way about you."

"Because deep down I know you're jealous of me, Brie."

"Jealous of what?"

"My not having to deal with idiots who judge me and having the freedom to explore my wildest desires. What's not to be jealous about? You're missing out, and you know it." Mary put an arm around her. "I actually feel sorry for you, Stinky Cheese."

Brie forcefully removed Mary's arm from her shoulder. "Just because this is right for you doesn't mean I would thrive here. I like knowing Sir and I are exclusive…for the most part," she added with a grin, reflecting on their threesome with Rytsar.

Mary crinkled her nose in disgust. "Being stuck with the same person for the rest of your life? I can't think of a worse punishment."

"I find knowing Sir on such an intimate level—one that no one else shares—is the greatest turn-on of all."

Mary patted Brie's cheeks, making a kissy face at her. "Oh, my poor little Brie, you're still such an innocent."

Brie pulled away from her, unamused. "I still maintain that you're the one who's secretly jealous. Face it—you can't stand the fact that I'm collared and you're not."

"As if… Faelan and I are having the time of our lives. Why would we ruin it with a collar?"

"You really don't want to wear his collar?" Brie asked, not quite believing it.

"Hell, no! It would feel like a noose around my neck."

"Well, I can't argue with you, because whatever you two are doing seems to be working. I'll admit, you seem more content than I thought possible."

Mary eyed her suspiciously. "What the hell do you mean by that?"

Brie laughed. "You seem sweet together…like an old married couple."

"Old married couple! Do you think you could be any more insulting, bitch?" Mary looked ready to deck her, but Brie didn't flinch.

"I actually meant it as a compliment, Mary."

"It's not!"

Brie rolled her eyes. "Okay, I take it back. You're not

sweet together."

Mary wasn't satisfied, and decided to throw Brie a curveball. "So what's the real story between you and Sir? Something's up, I can tell. Not everything is sweetness and light in Brieland."

Brie did not appreciate Mary's intuitive nature, and skirted the issue. "Both of us have been extremely busy, so that's made it hard to connect as much as we want."

"And?"

"And…things have happened."

Mary scooted closer. "Ooh, do tell! It's got to be juicy."

Brie wasn't about to expose herself to Blonde Nemesis after all her razzing. "Seriously, why would I tell you? It's obvious you'd just use it to harass me."

Mary frowned. "Hmm…you may be right. Let's forget all this sensitive, girly crap and talk about my scene."

Brie took a deep breath, reminding herself why she'd come to the commune. It wasn't about reconnecting with Mary, or Faelan, for that matter. Her sole purpose was to film segments for her documentary.

Although the scene Mary wanted to film would not be part of that, it might make the other participants more open to filming with her later.

"First, tell me where you plan to do this foursome, so I can plan how best to film around it."

Mary grinned, throwing her hands up in the air and gesturing to the sky. "Out here in the great outdoors."

Brie raised her eyebrow. "You? Out here in the open?"

"No, there is a perfect rock dubbed the Gang-Bang

Altar that's the perfect height for what we have planned."

"I think I need to see this legendary rock."

"I can take you there now," Mary said, standing up. "We can map it all out now so you won't distract me with stupid questions when the time comes."

As they walked through the woods, Brie asked her, "Todd mentioned an initiation for subs. Can you give me details, or is it a big secret?"

Mary's laugh was insulting. "It's not like we're part of a cult, Brie." She gave a wicked smile when she added, "The Initiation… OMG, it's the hottest thing ever. I swear every woman should experience it—including *you*."

"Fine, you've got me curious. Spill the beans."

"Before they can be accepted into the community, every submissive is required to go through the Initiation while his or her Dominant watches without participating."

"That sounds kinky."

"Trust me, it *is*." Mary spoke about it as if she were retelling a favorite fairytale. "First, you fast for twenty-four hours. Then they cleanse you to make you 'pure' for the community."

"What does the cleansing entail?"

"A bath, a thorough shave and an enema."

"I bet that enema was fun," Brie chuckled.

"*Everything* they do on that day is sensual and decadent," she insisted. "You're made to feel like a queen, with several attendants to take care of you for the day."

"So after you're made whole and pure, then what happens?"

"You're introduced to the community by your Dominant. He binds you to the ceremonial bed and then sits down to watch as you are tested."

"Tested? Okay, now you have my mouth watering."

Mary nodded. "I haven't even shared the best part. Your Dominant sits directly in front of you, so he can observe your reactions as every Dom in the commune scenes with you."

"What? Like a giant gang-bang?"

Mary shook her head slowly, a smile curling on her red lips. "Oh, no—they play with you one at a time with a specific goal in mind."

Brie felt goosebumps rise on her skin. "You're killing me, Mary. What's the goal?"

"Each Dom uses his unique set of skills to try to get you to orgasm, but the catch is that if you come, you will be punished."

Brie stopped walking in the middle of the trail to face her. "Holy crap. Did you come?"

Mary's smile grew wider. "I came again and again."

"On purpose?"

"Fuck, no! The punishments hurt like hell. But as much as I didn't want to, it just made my orgasms that much more intense. Knowing I was going to be severely punished each time I peaked with an orgasm…" She visibly shuddered. "Yeah, that's a feeling I'll never forget."

It was easy to see that Mary relished her memories of the experience, but then, the girl had been weird to begin with. "What kind of punishments, exactly?"

"Paddles, canes, nipple clamps, anal hooks, suspension, humiliation…you name it. They want it to hurt, because they want you to be scared when you orgasm."

Brie's heart raced at the thought. "I can't imagine. It sounds terrifying, but kinda hot too."

Mary patted her on the shoulder. "Even you, my wimpy friend, would love Initiation. Every Dom show-cases his or her skill on you, determined to make you orgasm in front of the community. In one night, I scened with every Dominant in the commune. The ceremony is pure genius!"

"Genius how?"

"I connected with every Dom on a personal level, experiencing their expertise as well as their favorite form of punishment. In one night, I became a real member of the community."

Brie could see how it was brilliant for the submissive, but what about their Dom? She imagined Faelan watching Mary orgasm under the hands of other Dominants, only to see her repeatedly punished for it.

"I don't understand what's in it for the initiate's Dominant. I mean, how did Todd benefit from it?"

"It's an honor to share your submissive with the commune, Brie," Mary said in a condescending tone. Then she elbowed her in the ribs, adding, "It also doesn't hurt that he gets to play with every future sub who joins the commune. Whereas we poor subs only get one glorious night, the Dominants get to join in every single Initiation."

"And you don't have a problem with that?"

"Why would I? It's only right that the new subs get to enjoy the same experience I had. And guess what?

We're having an Initiation next Friday. Although you're not allowed to film it, Faelan has already discussed it with Master Gannon, and he has no issues with you watching as long as you don't intervene in any way."

Brie kicked at a rock on the trail. "I wonder if I can handle it."

"Better bring a couple of towels. I'm telling you, Brie, you've never seen anything more erotic. Only thing sexier is being the lucky girl herself."

Brie realized she was far too possessive to ever enjoy it, but having the opportunity to watch? Well, that would be a rare treat indeed.

"After you see an Initiation, you won't want to leave here…"

That evening, Mary and Faelan asked Brie to join them at the communal fire after dinner. She had watched the entire commune come together and share a meal, talking and laughing like a giant family. Although no one spoke to her directly, there was still a feeling of belonging as she consumed the meal the community had grown, harvested and prepared together. Brie understood why Master Gannon insisted on these community dinners. It allowed the group to connect on a different, less formal level.

She joined Mary and Faelan behind the main building, around a giant fire pit encircled by rows of comfortable chairs. The group seemed even more relaxed and friendly as they shared stories and sang songs to the strum of a lone guitar.

It reminded Brie of nights spent at summer camp, except for one major difference. Throughout the night, couples openly played with each other. Some left the group to finish their scene alone, but most stayed by the fire to play in front of the group.

Brie watched covertly with lowered eyes as a couple beside her began their sexual dance. It started with a simple command for the sub to put her hands behind her back. The man ran his hands over her breasts, complimenting her on the feel of them. The woman moaned into Brie's ear, making her an accessory to their scene.

He nibbled on the sub's neck while he continued to massage her breasts. Brie saw his hand slip under her pants. The sub's wiggles and jerking motions let Brie know he was hitting just the right spot.

Soon the clothes became too limiting for him, and he slipped her pants down below her knees, commanding her to lean on Brie's chair for support. Brie continued to stare at the fire, but all her senses were focused on the couple. Brie soon heard the slippery sound of the sub's excitement as her Dom began pumping her with his fingers.

The woman purred into Brie's ear, begging him to use her. The Dom was cruelly playful and continued to stimulate his sub's clit with only his fingers, taking her close to climax without allowing her to come. It was not just his sub he was teasing, because the woman's close proximity and her eager noises had Brie just as invested in her sexual release.

Brie glanced to her left and saw that Mary and Faelan were playing with a female. Mary was kissing the girl passionately while Faelan used a small switch he'd found in the woods to make the sub squeal and wiggle as he whipped her fleshy ass.

Looking up at the bright stars twinkling in the clear mountain air, Brie thought this would be heaven on Earth if she wasn't alone and unplayed-with. To survive, she took on the attitude of a film director, noting the sounds and sights around her. Master Gannon had mentioned that she could film outside. If she could get a couple to agree, filming by the fire might prove the perfect way to capture the erotic nature of the outdoor play she was experiencing now.

She suddenly had an image of Rytsar taking her by the fire on the night of her first auction, and her pussy began to pulsate around the glass of her clit jewelry. Was it possible to come without any type of physical stimulation? Brie remembered how susceptible she was to games of the mind and suspected that if she wasn't careful she could unwillingly defy Sir's order not to orgasm, and on her very first night here.

Oh, the humiliation!

The sub on her right was commanded to straddle the Dom and their sexual dance became a rock-and-roll session. He thrust his cock deep into her as she rolled her hips in sensual circles, stimulating his shaft more intensely. The two let out groans of passion as they played with one another.

Brie diverted her attention back to Mary and Faelan,

which wasn't any help. Mary was under the girl, the two making out enthusiastically while Faelan plowed his cock into the sub. Both girls moved in unison to the rhythmic impact of his thrusting, which was a visual turn-on for Brie. The fact that Faelan stopped every now and then to admire the two girls and to play with Mary's clit was too much.

Brie stared at the fire, but the sounds of passion were impossible to ignore. She got up and hurried into the woods, needing the silence of the forest. However, she quickly stumbled on a noisy threesome and decided to head for the bridge, hoping the rushing water would drown out any sound.

What a wild place this commune was! Brie hadn't expected that she would be so profoundly affected by it. Being free to play without any judgment or restrictions really did make for an erotic environment. She looked up at the night sky. *More than ever, I'm missing you, Sir.*

Brie jumped when she felt something at her feet, then giggled when she saw it was only the black cat. "You scared me, big guy."

She picked up the large cat, surprised he wasn't heavier. She turned him to face her. "Are you made of just fur?" The cat meowed, so Brie cradled him in her arms and started to pet him, grateful for the company. His whole body vibrated with a deep purr.

The sound warmed Brie's heart, and the feelings of loneliness and desperation slowly eased. When her teeth started chattering from the cold night air, Brie put the cat down and made her way to Mary's bedroom.

To her delight, the cat followed her into the room

and jumped onto the bed. "I have something I have to do," she explained to the beast.

Brie took off all her clothes, except for the jewelry snug against her clit, and knelt on the floor, facing the direction of LA and her beloved Master. She placed her hands behind her back and thrust out her chest proudly for him.

She closed her eyes, imagining Sir standing in front of her. He had instructed her that the moment she felt his touch on her head, she could go to sleep. Brie concentrated on her vision of him, imagining him moving throughout his day, going to the meeting with his lawyer, eating meals alone, taking a hot shower to end the day... Her heart ached that she had missed that time with him. "I love you, Sir."

The instant the words left her lips, she felt the warmth of his touch on her head. She opened her eyes in surprise, half expecting to see him there. The room was empty, but his presence lingered with her.

Brie stood up and slipped under the covers, the black cat curling up beside her. She felt content on a level she hadn't expected. Sir had been right; this simple nightly protocol would bring her needed connection with him.

Mary came bounding in, scaring the cat out of the room. "Oh, my God, I love it here!" She let out a happy sigh as she started stripping in front of Brie. "So sad you can't partake of the fun, Stinky Cheese. Sure hope you brought your Hitachi, 'cause you're sure going to need it the next two weeks."

Heading off to the communal showers, Mary called behind her, "There's an outlet on the right side of the bed, just in case you feel the urge."

Brie wasn't about to tell Mary about her orgasm restriction. That girl would cause her no end of grief if she knew. Instead, Brie curled up, wrapping the blankets tightly around her. After a long day of travel and the activities of the commune, it didn't take long before she was sound asleep.

Mary's Triumph

Mary shook Brie. "Get up, sleepyhead!"

Brie grumbled and turned over, trying to ignore her. All week, the girl had been hounding Brie to get up at the break of dawn. Just once, she wanted the chance to sleep in, but Mary refused to leave her alone.

"You have to get up. I've arranged a breakfast with all the Doms who are scening with me today. I want them to feel comfortable around you, so you aren't a distraction during my scene."

When Brie didn't stir, Mary ripped off the blankets, exposing her to the cold mountain air. Brie scrambled to get the blankets back, but wasn't quick enough and finally conceded defeat, heading to the showers. Although Brie cherished her privacy, having communal showers had helped her to get to know a few of the other submissives.

"Hey, Ariel, how's that calf muscle?" she asked, knowing the girl had strained it in an extremely challenging suspension position the day before. Brie had filmed the outdoor session, enchanted that the Dom had used the branch of a tree as support.

The brunette pixie got on her tiptoes and did a ballerina twirl. "Good as new."

"I have to say, suspension in the wilderness certainly adds an element of magic to the whole experience."

Ariel smiled. "I do enjoy it whenever we have outdoor sessions. Being naked and bound in the warm sunlight is definitely arousing."

Brie looked down at her own white mound and laughed. "Unlike your tanned self, my pussy would have burned to a crisp with that kind of exposure."

Arial winked. "Oh, I remember the first time I experienced an intimate burn. Holy crap, that was intense!"

"Stop with all the jibber-jabber," Mary griped. "The men are waiting for us."

Brie hadn't seen Mary so anxious or excited before. She hoped the scene would live up to Mary's expectations and not end up being a painful disappointment recorded on film. Mr. Gallant had warned them during training that there were some fantasies that might seem erotic, but were really train-wrecks waiting to happen—and Mary was famous for her train-wrecks. Brie dreaded witnessing another one.

Mary's three Doms were eating breakfast at a table on the patio. Brie instantly recognized two of them. Rajah, one of the Gatekeepers she'd met on her first day, and the cowboy, Marcus, who had partaken of Mary's lips. The third man was a lean, dark African. The three men stood up as they approached, and for the first time since she'd been there, all three Doms acknowledged Brie by looking her directly in the eye. She instinctively wanted to lower hers, but realized that she needed to behave like a film director, not a sub. Brie met their gazes and smiled as she shook each of their hands.

"Thank you for allowing me to film you today, Rajah, Marcus and…"

The third Dom took her hand in both of his and nodded formally. "I am Kamau."

She bowed instinctively—she couldn't help herself. "Thank you, as well, Kamau."

The entire party sat down, with Mary placing herself in between two of the Doms, looking mighty pleased with herself.

Rajah took Mary's hand and turned it so her wrist was exposed. He lowered his head and bit down on it lightly as he stared at Brie with those mischievous green eyes. "We appreciate that our efforts will be recorded today. Not many women have the fortitude to attempt such a challenge."

"I can't wait," Mary said, her eyes flashing with lust and excitement.

Marcus asked Brie, "Will you be filming several different angles for us?"

"I plan to film three. Two stationary cameras will capture all the action, one from underneath while the other will focus on Mary's face to capture her reaction to your multiple attentions. I'll film the action as well, using a wider angle."

"Good," Kamau stated. "I want to see her expression when I fuck her in the ass with two cocks already buried inside her pussy."

Brie's stomach fluttered at the thought, but she remained professional as she explained, "The most important shot is capturing that moment when the head of your shaft breaches her entrance for the first time. Once I have that shot I will pull back to film the three of you thrusting into her." Brie's pussy responded just talking about the scene about to take place, and she felt a blush creep over her cheeks. "I also want to capture your individual facial expressions."

The three men looked at each other and nodded. Marcus spoke for them. "That's acceptable to us, Miss Bennett."

"Excellent." She turned to Mary. "Does that sound good to you?"

"Enough talk, already. I just want to get started, damn it."

Brie noticed that Mary hadn't eaten anything for breakfast, and assumed she was on a twenty-four hour fast to prepare herself for this three-cock invasion. While Brie liked the men well enough, there was no way she would ever have agreed to taking them all at once. However, she had a perverted sense of curiosity, wanting to know whether Mary would be able to handle them all.

The men finished their light meal, taking their time, knowing it was thoroughly testing Mary's patience. It was obvious to Brie that they enjoyed the power play.

To Mary's credit, she didn't hound the Doms to rush, but she kept glaring at Brie as if she were to blame.

Faelan came up before they were done and shook the hands of all three men before pulling up a chair to join them. "Is she chomping at the bit?"

Mary sat there silently while the men laughed.

"Foolish question, I know. This girl of mine hasn't talked about anything else for the past week."

"Do you plan to watch?" Brie asked him.

Faelan smiled, shaking his head. "No, this little stunt is between Mary and these fine gentlemen. However, I do plan to watch the video."

Brie wondered what Faelan was thinking. Was he really as okay with this scene as he appeared?

"It's something all of us have been looking forward to," Marcus said, touching the brim of his hat and nodding toward Mary.

The sexual tension between the group was palpable, and Brie found herself squirming in her seat because of it. It did not go unnoticed by Faelan, but he just winked at Brie. "Well, I will leave you all to your little experiment." He slapped Kamau on the back. "Be gentle with her—I want my girl back in one piece when you're done."

Faelan walked over to Mary, who stood up to receive his kiss. "Don't push yourself too far. You're more important than this little fantasy of yours." His eyes glinted with that wild look Brie had seen before as he ran his hand down Mary's front and cupped her pussy. "I consider this *my* property. Do not harm it."

Mary purred in pleasure.

Faelan gave her one last kiss before leaving the group to help round up the horses. Marcus was the first to stand and he offered Mary his hand. "Let's find out how much you can take, darlin'."

Brie ran to get her equipment and followed the foursome into the woods. Her heart was racing by the time they made it to Gang-Bang Altar. She felt almost as excited as Mary about the kinky scene about to take place.

As Brie set up the equipment, she found herself amazed that the rock truly looked as if it had been created with naughty sex in mind, with natural divots in the rock acting as hand-and-foot-holds to support different positions. She asked Mary to lie on the rock so she could get the right angle for both her stationary cameras. Once all her reflectors were set and adjusted, she announced to the group, "You can start any time. I won't speak, and will do my best to stay out of your way."

"Good," Mary said. "As far as I'm concerned, you don't exist." She ran her hands over the chests of all three men before taking the standing position of a sub ready to be commanded.

Marcus looked at Brie and tipped his hat, signifying that she was to begin filming. Brie trembled slightly when she hit *record*, focusing the camera on Mary. The three men removed their shirts before descending on her like hungry but well-mannered wolves—each one taking turns pulling at her clothing, sucking exposed parts and running their hands over her shapely body.

They circled Mary like predators as they played, all three men teasing her with their sexual caresses and forceful kisses. Brie moved slowly with them, catching the rawness of their lust and Mary's shameless enjoyment of it.

Mary moaned loudly while they played, inviting them to use her roughly. Brie noticed a change in their dynamic as the three men fed off each other's rising need for her. The air became more sexually charged as time went on.

Kamau was the first to strike, pulling Mary to him and ripping the last remnants of her panties away. He thrust his dark fingers inside her as he kissed her passionately. The other two watched as he finger-fucked her, forcing her first orgasm.

Kamau let go of her and Mary stumbled, struggling to remain on her feet. Marcus swooped in and picked her up, laying her on the rock and removing her remaining clothing. He stood back to admire her naked body. "Are you prepared to be ravished by three men, darlin'?"

She growled seductively and nodded.

Marcus pulled her arms above her head and began sucking on her breasts, before leaving a trail of kisses from her stomach down to the feminine swell of her mound. Marcus was more gentle than Kamau, but no less aggressive in his enjoyment of her. Mary squirmed and moaned, her passionate cry echoing in the woods when he induced a second orgasm with his tongue.

Rajah was the last to play with her. He took her left wrist and lifted her arm, nibbling and biting down the length of it. Mary squealed when his teeth landed on her nipple. He chuckled, leaving a new trail of bite marks from her breast to her hip bone. By then, Mary was visibly trembling with desire.

He lifted her from the altar and told her to stand, being careful not to knock over the camera as he took off his clothes and lay down on it, motioning Mary to him. "Wet my *lund* with that needy *chut*," he growled huskily.

Mary used the natural divots in the rock to climb back up and straddle him. She coated his shaft with her eagerness, grinding shamelessly against his cock. He aided her by grabbing her ass cheeks with both hands and sliding Mary's dripping pussy up and down on his rigid shaft.

Meanwhile, the other two men undressed themselves and started stroking their cocks in anticipation. After Brie caught them on film, she focused back on Mary, certain the first penetration was close at hand.

Rajah held his cock in position as Mary slowly descended onto it. She groaned with pleasure when his lengthy shaft slipped inside. He gripped her ass, forcing her up and down on his stiff rod, then held her still, commanding her to grind harder. "Do not stop until you come."

Mary was in control of the speed of his cock rubbing against her mound, but Brie knew the pressure he was placing on her clit was making it far more intense. Mary braced herself and started grinding hard and fast. Rajah lifted his head and bit her neck.

Mary moaned passionately, "Ooh…ooh…OOH!"

Wetness covered his balls, announcing her third orgasm to the world. Brie pulled the shot back as Marcus moved into position between her legs.

Mary's pussy was glistening and swollen, making it slippery and ready for Marcus' unnatural invasion. "You're going to take all of me, darlin'." He held on to his shaft and began pressing against her full cunt. He rocked his cock against her, pressing even harder. Brie held her breath, wondering what it must feel like and if it was similar to taking Boa's massive shaft.

"Harder; I need it harder," Mary begged.

Marcus' shaft slowly stretched and then breached her resistant hole. She moaned loudly as he pushed in deeper. The two men coordinated their thrusts, pushing into her as one unit. Rajah grabbed her hips as support as he thrust deeper.

Mary began crying loudly, "Fuck yeah! Oh, fuck yeah…"

Kamau was the last, but before he mounted her, he asked, "How does it feel?"

She panted. "God…it's amazing… Feels like…I'm being ripped in two…but I fucking love it!"

"Are you ready for a third?"

She tilted her head back and offered him her lips as the other two continued to fuck her overstretched pussy with rhythmic thrusts. Kamau traced her lips with his tongue before kissing her deeply.

"And now I am going to make your fantasy complete." Kamau launched himself onto the rock with the grace of a gazelle. His was the hardest position, because he had to straddle Mary without getting in the way of Marcus, but this man was incredibly limber.

He got into position, stroking his lubricant-covered cock. It was deliciously dark, with a round head and long, thin shaft. Brie felt tingles course through her as he pressed the head of it against Mary's bright pink rosette.

Marcus directed Kamau verbally to ensure he got the proper angle. "Lower. Right there, you got it, you got it…"

Brie gasped softly when she saw his dark shaft slowly slip into Mary's tight ass.

Rajah groaned as he gripped Mary's buttocks. She tilted her head back and cried, "Oh, yes! Oh, my God, yes!"

Kamau grabbed her hair, using her to brace himself for better control. "Can you take more?"

"Fuck, yeah..."

He tried to push deeper into her, but her body resisted and he made no progress. It took the coordination of all three men to get his shaft to sink in farther. The excitement of the group was tangible.

Marcus grasped Mary's thighs. "You look sweet all filled up, darlin', but now we're going to make you scream."

"Do it, do it," Mary begged.

Brie had stopped breathing at this point, her heart pounding in her chest as the three men started thrusting into Mary.

Mary let out a low, primal moan that sounded more animal than human. The three men continued fucking her, their grunts of satisfaction and effort echoing in the woods as they worked together to ensure the deepest penetration. Brie watched in fascination as Mary's body accepted the onslaught, her ass muscles clutching onto Kamau's dark shaft, seeming unwilling to let it go whenever he pulled back.

Soon the woods filled with Mary's screams.

The men slowed their strokes, and Rajah kissed Mary. "So sexy..." he murmured. Her whole body relaxed as she started to fly, allowing them to take her even more deeply.

Kamau came first. Lifting his head, he let out a warrior's cry as he orgasmed. He pulled out his dark shaft, a gush of white liquid dripping from her stretched ass. Marcus pulled out and commanded Mary to play with his balls as he squeezed her buttocks together and fucked the valley of her ass. Her perfectly manicured nails grasped his balls as he let loose, his essence covering her entire back.

Rajah now had free access to her pussy and grabbed her buttocks with both hands, pumping her hard as he came. His guttural cries affected Brie, causing her clit to throb against her jewelry.

The two other men helped Mary off Rajah and lay her on the altar. They caressed her skin, giving her light kisses as they praised her accomplishment. She was unable to speak, but Brie could see the smile on her face from where she stood. She zoomed in, knowing Mary probably wouldn't remember this part of the scene.

The care and respect shown to her by the three men was touching, and demonstrated to Brie how much the community at the Sanctuary cared for one another. She stopped filming and quietly put her equipment away, not wanting to disturb Mary's aftercare.

Marcus tipped his hat to her as she left. She smiled and nodded, knowing that she would once again become a ghost to him now that the scene was over. She accepted her fate, grateful for this glimpse into their intimate world.

The Initiation

B rie had been anticipating the Initiation ever since
Mary mentioned it. The idea of every Dom participating in the ceremony completely blew her mind.

Initiation was a huge deal for the community. Instead
of having a communal dinner, the group gathered for
breakfast, knowing that the evening would be taken up
by the event. Every person there seemed energized, eager
to bring two new members into the fold.

Faelan had explained to Brie that the community was
in charge of culling the applicants to a select few, but it
was up to Master Gannon to make the final decision. It
meant no one knew who was going to walk through the
gate to join their extended family except Gannon.

Brie wasn't allowed to participate in the preparations,
but the moment the room was ready, Mary dragged her
in to see it. When Brie stepped into the main room, she
had to stop for a moment to take it all in. The huge
room had been completely transformed.

In the center was a four-poster bed. It was opulent,
with carved wooden posts and gossamer material flowing

from the top of each post in a canopy of white. The bed itself was covered in a virginal white coverlet with a variety of uniquely shaped pillows to aid in various sexual positions.

To the right were several tables covered in different tools, running the gamut of BDSM play. On the left were common pieces of kinky furniture, including a tantra chair, a spanking bench, and an iron cage.

Just behind the bed sat an impressive throne, intricately carved, with upholstery of rich red velvet. Mary led her over and told her to stand beside it. "This way we get to see all the action up close. If you want a good spot, you have to come early or you'll end up standing in the back and missing all the good stuff."

"Is there anything I'm expected to do?"

"You're only here to observe. That means no talking, and if you must leave, you'll need to go through the back." She pointed in the direction of the kitchen. "It's common for couples to leave for a temporary break throughout the ceremony."

"I bet it is."

"Actually, it's expected and encouraged, but not for poor Brianna Bennett. She gets to stand here through the whole ceremony and burst into flames, a victim of spontaneous human combustion."

Brie hit Mary's arm. "That's the part I am *not* looking forward to. So how long does an Initiation take?"

"Hours and hours…"

"Oh, great."

Mary opened the large purse she was carrying. "That's why I brought plenty of water and," she pulled out a small hand towel, "something for you."

Brie laughed. "Thanks for thinking of me."

"No problem. Feel free to wipe your snatch whenever you feel the need."

Brie stuffed the towel back in Mary's bag when she saw Faelan approaching through the gathering crowd. "I'm sure I'll be fine."

But Blonde Nemesis wasn't letting her go that easily. "No really, if you want you can stand on the towel. That way you won't get the floor all messy, little Miss Moist-a-Lot."

Brie elbowed Mary. "You suck."

"Better than you…"

Brie didn't miss Faelan's amused snort, and she protested, "I'm positive Sir would disagree."

"Oh, really?" Mary laughed. "Why don't we ask him? He certainly seemed to enjoy my lips during training."

Brie had never forgotten being forced to watch Mary go down on Sir when she'd had the DP session with Master Coen, but Brie pretended she didn't care and answered lightly, "Obviously Sir preferred my lips, and that's why I'm collared."

Mary raised her eyebrows. "You wear that thing as if it's something to be proud of."

Brie fingered her collar and smiled knowingly. "Jealous…"

Mary hit Faelan in the shoulder. "I told you she was an idiot."

"It's not our place to judge," he replied, standing behind Mary and putting his hands on her shoulders. Mary rolled her eyes in irritation.

"I saw that," he stated. "Should I make you do a set of twenty?"

Mary shook her head.

"Fine. Apologize for rolling your eyes and disrespecting your friend."

Mary's jaw fell open.

"Drop or speak, it's your choice."

Mary sighed in frustration, but complied. "I'm sorry for rolling my eyes, although I have no idea how you saw it, and—"

Everyone suddenly became silent around them as the crowd turned to face the large doors. Brie followed their gaze and watched as the new couple entered the room.

"That's the initiate," Mary whispered with reverence.

Brie watched the curvaceous woman in a bright crimson dress walk into the room escorted by her Dom, who was dressed in a black tux. She murmured, "I didn't expect it would be so formal."

Faelan whispered, "This is their chance to impress us."

Brie looked at the woman again, with her perfect hair, perfect red lips and those ample breasts spilling out of her tight bodice.

Well, I'm impressed.

The Dom led his submissive to the large bed and pulled her head back roughly, kissing her on the forehead before picking her up. He lay her on the bed and began tying her to the posts using quick, skillful knots.

It looked to Brie as if the initiate were being presented as a sacrifice. She could feel the excitement in the room rise, every eye on the couple.

Once the submissive was secure, her Dom turned to the group. Brie breathed in sharply and felt Mary stiffen beside her. The man was older, with sharp features and cold, hard eyes. His intimidating confidence gave Brie chills.

He announced to the assembly in a gruff voice, "I am Razor. This is my submissive, null. I give her to you tonight as a sign of my trust, and her willingness to please."

Brie did not care for the pet name of Razor's submissive, but understood its meaning. The submissive was nothing, and Brie suspected the Dominant was null's chosen instrument of pain.

Brie couldn't help shuddering as he approached, and lowered her eyes when he glanced in her direction before sitting down. She suddenly wished Mary hadn't insisted on standing so close to the throne. The fierceness of his confidence rolled off the man in waves, making it hard for her to concentrate. She noticed that Mary was equally affected, and was not surprised when Faelan instinctively wrapped his arms around his woman.

The dramatic sound of a large drum announced the beginning of the ceremony. It gave a welcome solemnness to the occasion. When it stopped, all eyes turned to their leader.

Master Gannon spoke to the community in a somber voice. "We accept the gift of your submissive tonight, Razor. We promise to instruct her well in the practice of self-denial."

Razor replied, "May she prove worthy of your attention."

Master Gannon removed his shirt before picking up a cane. "I am Master Gannon, null. I am the leader of this commune. Tonight you will be challenged by each of the Dominants, but you retain the right to stop an activity with the safeword 'red'. What is your safeword?"

"Red, Master Gannon."

"Very good. Then let us begin. You are not allowed to orgasm, null. Disobedience in this area will be met with immediate and severe punishment. Do you understand?"

Brie was close enough to see the bound sub's chest rising and falling rapidly, but she nodded as she answered, "I will obey, Master Gannon."

He snorted. "I *will* make you come."

Mary let out a sigh beside Brie, and whispered, "Yes, he will…"

Master Gannon placed the cane in null's mouth. "Hold this until I punish you."

He went to the table and picked up two clover nipple clamps. Brie knew they were the most painful kind of clamps. He also grabbed some weights, tossing them in his hand as he approached.

"I heard you like these."

The sub nodded lustfully.

He knelt on the bed and unbuttoned her bodice, pulling the material down to expose her large breasts. He massaged and teased them before he attached the first clamp to her nipple. The girl remained silent, giving no indication of the intense pressure the tool provided. He bent down and sucked on her other nipple before attaching the second clamp.

Master Gannon then undid the bindings and had her stand up for him, the cane still in her mouth. He tied her wrists together and bound them above her head to one of the foot posts of the canopy bed. He smiled seductively as he added weights to each clamp.

Null whimpered softly in response.

"Now that I have you primed, I am going to make you orgasm."

He knelt down on one knee and pulled off her panties, having her step out of them. He took the bottom hem of her dress and tucked it inside her open bodice to expose her shaved pussy to the community.

"Open those pretty legs," he commanded.

Null obeyed, spreading her legs apart as she balanced in her high heels. Master Gannon looked up at her and said forcefully, "Do *not* come."

Mary nudged Brie, the smile on her face letting Brie know the girl was about to disobey that direct order.

The voluptuous sub moaned when Master Gannon began playing with her pussy. When he had enough natural lubricant covering his fingers, he forced three inside and began pumping inside her in an almost violent manner. The aggressiveness of his hand quickly produced wet sounds as her body unwillingly gave in to the stimulation. Null threw her head back and let out a low cry that quickly increased in pitch. She groaned against the cane in her mouth as her sex pulsated and a huge gush of watery fluid escaped from her slick pussy.

Master Gannon stood up and walked over to the table, casually wiping his hand on a towel as he stared at her. She stood there squirming under his forceful gaze when he approached.

"Open."

She parted her lips and the cane fell into his hand.

As he pulled off the nipple clamps, Brie saw null grimace in pain but she made no sound. Then he untied her wrists and asked, "What did I tell you?"

"That I would be punished if I came."

"Bend over the bed so that you are facing your Master. Lift your skirt and take your punishment."

Null looked at Razor briefly and then quickly lowered her eyes. He wore a slight smirk on his lips as she bent over and lifted her skirt for Master Gannon.

The commune leader stood behind her, the cane cocked and ready. Gannon rubbed the soft swell of her ass appreciatively as he explained, "I will be quick and thorough." With that, he whipped the cane repeatedly across her ass. Null whimpered and squirmed, only crying out twice. Afterwards, he caressed the welts he had left before commanding her to stand.

Master Gannon cupped her chin and kissed her on the lips, telling null, "See that you learn your lesson well tonight."

He walked over to take a place in the crowd, while another Dom took his place with null. This man was dressed in black jeans and a dark shirt with a breast pocket, the sleeves of which had been rolled up to show off his tattoos. Although Brie had not met him personally, she'd been told he was the resident blacksmith. He certainly fit the part, with his large arms and rough five o'clock shadow.

He approached the sub with a serious expression

that let her know he was not one to be trifled with. "You will call me Wayland. You are not allowed to orgasm. Disobedience will result in immediate and severe punishment. Do you understand, null?"

She nodded, but her voice wasn't as certain as it had been the first time when she answered, "I will obey, Wayland."

He pulled at her bodice to more fully expose her breasts to the crowd before ordering, "Move over to the spanking bench."

She shuddered, her ass already red and painful from her first punishment, but dutifully walked over to the bench.

"Mount it and bare your ass to me."

Null climbed onto the furniture and pulled up her dress, showing off the marks left by the cane.

"I like my submissives to feel helpless. I want them to know there is nothing to stop me from taking my pleasure." Wayland went to the table and returned with an anal hook. He smiled as he held it up to her. "I made this one myself. I was told you are familiar with the tool."

Null answered, "I am, Wayland."

"Good." He coated the metal tool with a liquid lubricant and stood beside her, separating her ass cheeks with his other hand. "I made the end extra-large. Do you think you can take it?"

She looked behind her at the round ball at the end of the large hook—the part that was to go inside her—and nodded.

"Let's see if you're right. You may want to bear

down for this one." He used his strong arm muscles to slowly force the large metal ball inside her ass. Null took it, purring as the huge ball finally slipped inside.

"You do like these, don't you?" Wayland complimented. He twisted up her hair into a long rope with his hand and secured it with a leather strip. He tied the rope of her hair to the anal hook and tightened it so she had to keep her head back in the stretched position.

Wayland took out a cigar from his breast pocket and lit it, breathing in the smoke and slowly exhaling as he watched her strain in her bonds. He stared at her amorously for several moments before moving to her head and squatting so his lips were level with hers, just inches from her face. "Breathe in," he commanded.

Wayland slowly exhaled, and the wisps of smoke seductively swirled between them as null breathed it in. Brie couldn't believe how sensual the simple act was, and shifted uncomfortably where she stood.

He stood back up and picked up a vibrator that looked suspiciously like a mini Hitachi wand from the table. He placed the buzzing vibrator against her clit. Null struggled, but the anal hook effectively kept her in place. He slowly moved it up and down her clit, reminding her that the punishment would be great if she came. Null started whimpering and then cried out in fear when her body betrayed her and her pussy pulsed against the wicked toy.

Wayland immediately turned it off, saying nothing as he put the vibrator down. Before he punished her, he meticulously cleaned all her exposed skin. Then he walked back to the table and put on a thick leather glove, sliding a white plastic container next to the bench with his foot. "As a blacksmith, I have a particular attraction to burning metal." White mist rose out of the bucket when he opened the lid. He pulled out a metal rod with a brand on the end and approached her. "I will not leave a permanent mark, but you will experience the burn."

Null looked at him, her eyes wide with fear, but she was helpless to avoid her punishment.

"Why are you being punished, null?"

"I disobeyed your command and came, Wayland."

Wayland nodded. "Yes, you did, and now you must pay." He branded her left ass cheek first, leaving the brand there for several seconds. The sizzling sound of cold metal meeting skin made Brie tingle with excitement and fear, remembering her own branding.

Wayland picked up another brand from the bucket. Null looked at him wildly as he moved to face her, the brand inches from her face. "No, I would never mark that beautiful face," he assured her.

He placed the brand on her exposed breast, chuckling softly to himself when she whimpered. "It burns, doesn't it?"

Brie noticed that Wayland was careful to press the brand only lightly, leaving it there for just a few seconds so she would feel the burn but it would not permanently harm the skin. He moved around her, branding different areas, leaving her right buttock for last. "Learn your lesson well tonight." He pressed it against her ass, leaving it on a little longer so she would not forget.

Brie noticed the woman's increased breath, and understood that null was breathing through the discomfort.

When he'd finished, he knelt and kissed her. "You received your punishment well, null."

While she was still quivering from her last orgasm and punishment, Faelan left Mary's side and approached the spanking bench. "You will call me Faelan. You are not allowed to orgasm. Disobedience will result in immediate and severe punishment. Do you understand, null?"

She looked up at him and swallowed hard. "I will obey, Faelan."

He smiled at her charmingly as he undid her bindings and removed the hook. "I'm sure you will try."

The girl trembled, but her eyes were locked on him. Brie could tell she was already under Faelan's spell. Brie glanced over at Mary, surprised to see her staring at Razor instead of watching the scene. Brie bumped shoulders with her, and Mary jumped as if being caught doing something wrong. Brie gave her a questioning look.

Mary responded by mouthing the word, "bitch".

What the hell is your problem? Brie wondered, shrugging it off.

She chose to ignore Mary and focused her attention back on Faelan. He'd freed null of her dress and laid her on the bed. He unbuttoned his shirt slowly before taking it off, making her wait for him to begin.

The boy had grown in confidence and skill since Brie had scened with him at the Center, but Faelan still maintained that primal element that brought out the animal in a woman. There was no doubt he held that power over null as she panted and growled, inviting his rough play.

The poor girl was completely captivated when Faelan brought out the knife and began teasing her with it, pressing the sharp edge of it against her most sensitive areas and dragging it across her skin with enough pressure to scratch, but not to break the surface. Her eyes were wide and her breaths shallow as she watched the deadly knife caress her skin.

"Are you scared?" he asked.

She looked at him with trembling lips, and nodded.

He brought the knife up to her neck, pressing it against her jugular. "You should be."

With the rush of adrenaline caused by the edge play, Brie knew it wouldn't take much to send null over the brink. She watched in anticipation as he dragged the knife back down over her curvaceous body, ending at her swollen mound.

"Do you know what I am about to do?" he asked.

Null answered hesitantly, "Make me come?"

Faelan moved between her legs, grinning when he confirmed her answer. "Yes, null." He pressed the point of the knife to the top of her mound. "If you move, you will cut yourself."

With that warning hanging in the air, Faelan began to eat her pussy, relentlessly applying that skilled tongue to her erect clit.

The danger of the knife had null on such a sub high that she came almost instantly.

Faelan pulled back, a charming smirk on his lips. "Null, you disappoint me."

"I'm sorry, Faelan."

"Although I accept your apology, it is my duty to punish you." He left the bed to get his chosen tool of punishment, a violet wand. The way null stared nervously at the instrument let Brie know she was very familiar with it.

Null looked up at him repentantly, quietly accepting her fate.

"Stand in front of your Master," Faelan commanded.

She followed his order, but kept her head down as she faced Razor.

"Look him in the eye, null."

She slowly raised her head and stared bravely into the eyes of her intimidating Master. Brie could only imagine what she was feeling.

Faelan stood behind the sub and turned on the device. The crackling sound of the wand added an element of danger to the punishment scene.

"I can tell you are a dedicated sub, null," Faelan growled into her ear, "even though you disobeyed a direct command."

Brie appreciated that Faelan was giving null words of empowerment, even though she had failed in her task—a task she was *meant* to fail.

Faelan turned up the intensity of the wand before touching her with it. Null involuntarily flinched, but stayed in place. He dragged it down from her ribs to her hip, stating, "It feels like the edge of a knife cutting into you, doesn't it?"

She nodded, looking nervously to her left, anticipating the next pass. He did not disappoint, shocking her sensitive skin with the intense current. He held her to him as he made a pattern of concentric circles on her belly. Brie could see her muscles contracting as they came into contact with the stinging instrument.

Faelan turned off the wand and a profound silence followed. He kissed her neck gently and murmured, "Your pussy looks neglected, null."

She stiffened in his arms when the buzzing started up again. Faelan wrapped his arm firmly around her waist and brought the wand to within an inch of her swollen mound. He waited several moments before he grazed it against her clit.

Null let out a frightened gasp but made no more sound, gritting her teeth and accepting the sting of the instrument without complaint.

"Good null…" he said, shutting off the device. He turned her chin towards him and kissed her deeply. Brie did not miss her passionate whimper when he broke away.

Faelan returned to Mary, obviously turned on by the scene he'd just finished. He ran his hands over her body while nibbling on her ear whispering nasty things to her. Before long, Mary was dragging him through the crowd, towards the back door.

Brie sighed in frustration, attracting the attention of Razor. He glanced up at her with those dangerous, steel-blue eyes and she stopped breathing for a moment. He was all kinds of scary.

Without the reassuring presence of Mary and Faelan, Brie decided to leave the ceremony. She escaped to Mary's room, where she undressed and crawled into bed after performing her assigned nightly ritual.

Sir's presence seemed to remain in the room, tempting her. Brie was excited by the activities she'd witnessed and slipped her finger between her legs, stroking her clit jewelry. "Oh, Sir, if only you were here."

The subtle throbbing was tempting her like a siren's call to let go and stop the terrible ache in her loins.

Just a little more pressure…

The creak of the door stopped her cold. With her heart pounding in her chest, Brie opened her eyes and saw the door ajar, but no one standing in the doorway. She sighed in relief, but let out a squeal of terror when the black cat jumped on her bed.

"Oh, thank goodness it's just you!" she cried, holding out her hand to the cat. He sauntered slowly up to her, rubbing his cheek against her in a possessive manner. She gathered him in her arms, laughing at herself. "You scared me to death, you bad, bad boy."

He began purring, oblivious of the fright he'd just given her.

Brie scratched him under the chin, grateful for the distraction. "I guess I should thank you. You just saved me from disobeying my Master."

Her Challenge

B rie was surprised when Rajah came up to her during breakfast and told her that she needed to meet with Master Gannon directly. She excused herself, giving Mary a confused look before she followed Rajah to Gannon's office.

"Miss Bennett, please sit down."

She sat, folding her hands in her lap to hide her nervousness. "What's this about, Gannon?"

"I normally do not allow phone calls, but Sir Davis has asked to speak to you. Because of the unusual circumstances, I have granted him the favor. You may call him on my private phone. Get me when you're done."

It felt as if the ground was falling out from under her. Something bad had happened to Sir's mother, she was sure of it. However, she kept her voice calm as she took the phone from him. "Thank you, Gannon."

He left the room, shutting the door quietly behind him.

Brie stared at the phone, afraid to make the call to Sir

but dutifully calling nonetheless. Her stomach fluttered on hearing his voice.

"Hello, this is Thane Davis."

"Sir."

"Ah, Brie. It's good to hear from you."

"Is everything all right?" she asked uneasily.

"Yes, babygirl. There's no need to be concerned."

"Then why the phone call, Sir?"

"Gannon contacted me a few days ago and made a suggestion that I have been mulling over. I've decided you would benefit from the experience and have given him my permission."

She felt a thrill of excitement. "Permission for what, Sir?"

"I've been told they are having a dungeon event."

"Yes, it's tonight! It's a quarterly event at the Sanctuary. Quite the to-do I've been told."

"Tell me more."

She smiled, happy to share the details with him. "They transform their main room into a dungeon, and give each of the subs a role to play."

"What kinds of roles?"

"Some get to clean the equipment after each use, a few serve food and drink throughout the event, there's even a group who act as toys, but the rest get to be dungeon playmates."

"It sounds like an interesting setup."

"I agree, Sir. I was afraid I'd have to miss out, because I hadn't even been invited to observe the event."

"Gannon firmly believes you cannot fully appreciate the importance of what the Sanctuary provides to its community unless you are a participating member, and he does not want you leaving there without getting a taste of his vision."

"Did he tell you how he wanted me to participate tonight?"

"He did, Brie."

She giggled nervously when he did not explain further. "And how am I to participate, Sir?"

"It will be a challenge for you, téa."

Her heart raced when he used her sub name. "What is being asked of me, Master?"

"You will act as a toy tonight."

She couldn't breathe. It was the last thing she'd expected to hear. "I'm not sure I can. I mean—"

"Think of this the same way as you would a lesson at the Center. I want you to experience something you've never faced before and learn from it."

"But Sir, the toys are open to all the Dominants of the commune."

"I want you to be aware that I've spoken to Gannon about Wallace and you will be off-limits to him."

Although Brie was relieved to hear it, she still struggled with the idea of taking on the role of a toy. "Master…"

"I believe you will gain valuable insight from this experience, téa. I am commanding you to present yourself tonight for the festivities. I want you to embrace it, to relish it for the once-in-a-lifetime encounter it is."

Brie swallowed hard, choking on the lump that had suddenly formed in her throat. This felt exactly like the time he'd asked her to serve under a new Master. She whispered into the phone, "What if I say no?"

"I will be very disappointed."

His words cut her like a knife. She didn't want to refuse him, but to give herself away like that…

"Brie, you *must* trust me."

Calling her given name had great power over her. Sir was asking her to trust him on a deeper level, as her Master *and* partner.

Brie closed her eyes. Did she trust Sir to further her submissive journey—or not?

While she did trust him, it was with great reservation that she answered, "I will do as you ask, but only if it pleases you."

He laughed, knowing she was politely voicing her unwillingness. "It *does* please me, téa," he assured her.

"Then I will join the event, Sir, because that is what you have commanded of me."

"Don't just *do* it, Brie. I want you to give yourself over fully to it, as if you were giving yourself to me. I want your pussy dripping with anticipation for any hand that touches you."

She trembled listening to his directive. His words made her long to please him, to embrace her role as a plaything, to make him proud of her service even though it would be in the hands of another.

"What are you going to do for me tonight, Brie?" Sir asked, making her voice his command out loud for his benefit—and hers.

She took a deep breath to calm the butterflies in her stomach. "I am going to please the Dominants with the same enthusiasm I reserve for you, Sir."

"Yes," he growled seductively. "Hold nothing back. I expect a full account when I speak with you next."

Brie let out an uneasy sigh as she hung up.

Would she truly be able to give herself over in both mind and body to fulfill Sir's challenging command? For the first time since being collared, Brie was haunted by a sense of doubt, worried she might fail.

Brie was grateful for Mary in a time like this. If there was anyone who could snap her into the proper frame of mind to play out her assigned role, it was Blonde Nemesis.

Because so many subs were preparing for the dungeon event, Brie and Mary had to shower in the same stall together. Although Brie had seen Mary naked plenty of times, it was a little odd when they kept touching as they soaped up.

It didn't help things when Brie felt Mary's hand rub against her pussy. "Be sure to lather up good there. It's going to be used a lot tonight."

Brie automatically smacked her hand away before pushing her out of the stall. Mary screamed and scrambled back in, throwing Brie up against the shower stall. "What the fuck, bitch?"

"You freakin' touched my snatch! I don't remember giving you permission to touch it."

"Oh, my God, Brie. It's not like it's the eighth wonder of the world. Hey, everyone, I touched Brie's cooch, now I'm eternally blessed."

The subs in the other shower stalls started laughing hysterically.

"Screw you, Mary." Brie couldn't help it; she joined in their laughter. "But for future reference, my sacred pussy is off-limits to the likes of *you*."

Mary rolled her eyes as she rubbed the bar of soap over her tanned breasts. The rest of their shared shower experience was performed in silence, but the two snuck amused looks at each other while the rest of the subs continued to break out in spontaneous giggles.

As Brie toweled off, she glanced around and noticed that the other subs, both male and female, had perfect tans. Nude sunbathing seemed to be the norm at the commune and their even skin tones certainly made for a pleasant look. Brie glanced down at her swimsuit lines, realizing she would stand out among the others tonight looking *very* vanilla.

However, she knew confidence was key as a submissive. Instead of seeing it as a liability, she decided to embrace her multi-shading. It made her unique, a rarity among the submissives here. She wasn't one of them, which would make her more attractive to some of the Dominants.

Brie still hadn't gotten used to the fact that none of the Doms had looked at her in a sexual way since she'd entered the commune. She understood the reasons why, but hadn't realized until now how much she depended on that sexual tension to give her energy. Being a ghost was not freeing for her. On the contrary, it had proven to be completely exhausting.

"Girls, as you know, this is Brie's first time as a toy. Any advice for her?" Mary asked, in a show of unexpected kindness.

One of the girls answered, "Being a toy always takes me into subspace. There is just something about being treated roughly with no regard that's a total turn-on for me."

"Yeah, I second that," an older woman agreed. "I like the feeling of being used. You mean nothing and everything to them in that moment, simply for the release your body can provide."

"That's sexy to you?" Brie asked.

"Objectification is hot. Have you tried it?"

"I was a platter once."

All of the submissives chuckled at her answer— really, she couldn't blame them.

"A platter, huh? Well, you aren't going to be experiencing platter action tonight, little girl," a male chimed in, snapping his towel on Brie's ass.

Brie squealed and the group laughed again.

"Enough of this racket," Master Gannon barked, walking in on the group.

For a fraction of a second, Brie almost covered herself with her hands, but resisted the urge when she noticed everyone standing to attention. She straightened her back and put her hands to her sides in an open and inviting manner.

"The dungeon is nearly ready. Have yourselves prepared to join me in five minutes." He looked briefly at Brie, infusing her with a sense of responsibility and excitement. This wasn't just about her experiencing objectification for her own benefit; her role tonight was to please the Doms of the commune who would partake of her.

"You will be on the farthest end, Miss Bennett."

She nodded and looked at her feet, a feeling of exhilaration coursing through her for the first time. This truly was something she had never experienced—never dreamed of experiencing.

In order to honor Sir's command to give herself over to this with no reservations, she knew she had to change her state of mind and told herself, *I am a submissive. My very nature is to serve, and I'm being asked to serve the Dominants of this commune. It is my pleasure to serve and please them. I will embrace my duty with an open mind and full heart. This is what my Master commands of me. This is his desire—and mine.*

Mary bumped her shoulder. "It's time. Hell, this may be the most exciting thing you ever do, Brie."

The interior of the lodge had been completely altered. The long sectional couch in the middle was gone, replaced by all kinds of different play furniture from spanking benches, whipping posts and St Andrew's crosses to wooden A-frames and cages. Some of the furniture Brie had never seen before, and could only guess at its use. There were also rows of tables with various tools spread out, and areas specifically set aside for aftercare. Brie liked the light, airy, spacious feel of this particular dungeon environment.

"You will proceed to the beds," Gannon instructed, pointing to the row of beds lined against the farthest wall. They all had iron headboards, but these beds were thinner than a normal twin and each was covered in a plastic sheet. It was obvious their sole purpose was for fucking.

Brie's stomach fluttered when she noticed the strands of red rope that had been placed on each bed. The last one—the one meant for her—also had a small table beside it, with lubricant and a variety of condoms laid out.

Brie was grateful that Mary came up from behind and chose the bed beside hers. Doing this challenge was intimidating but having a friend there, even if it was Mary, gave her more confidence.

The naked submissives each stood at the foot of a bed, hands behind their backs, legs spread apart, patiently waiting their turn. Brie quickly followed suit. Naturally, Master Gannon started with the girl on the other end.

Brie watched covertly as the sub was commanded to lie on the bed on her back with her head at the edge. Brie had to smile; it was the perfect height to offer oral stimulation. The girl's wrists were secured to the legs of the bed. He then moved to the headboard and told her to spread her legs. With rapid movements, he tied her ankles to the metal. Master Gannon returned to the end of the bed and gently smacked her cheek before leaving her. "Good girl…"

The first toy was bound and ready for play.

The King Returns

Master Gannon moved on to the next submissive, who happened to be the male who'd snapped Brie's ass with a towel. He was ordered to lie on his back, with his wrists resting against the headboard. Gannon secured them tightly, then bound his ankles to the legs of the bed. Just that simple contact of being bound had the submissive's cock rising to attention. Gannon slapped the sub's masculine thigh before moving on.

Each submissive was tied into a different position so that the Dominants would have their choice of play without having to remove or change the rope bindings.

When Master Gannon finally reached Brie, she was a quivering mess of nerves. This was it—she was about to become a toy.

Unlike with the other submissives, Master Gannon talked to her before he began. "Are you prepared for this, Miss Bennett?"

She nodded. "I am, Gannon."

"You will not be released from your bonds until the end of the play session. This is not only a test of your submissive nature, but your endurance. We do not choose our toys lightly. Consider this an extreme honor."

His words helped her to focus on what was being asked of her, and she answered confidently, "I do, Gannon."

He pulled out a sash from his jeans pocket. "Turn."

Brie was surprised and wondered if she was being blindfolded because she was not a member of the commune. Thankfully, blindfolds gave her a sense of power, and she accepted it graciously.

"On the bed, toy, with your knees under your torso."

She felt for the bed and settled down onto it, tucking her knees in, knowing the position lifted her buttocks at a pleasing angle to allow access to both her pussy and ass.

Master Gannon took her left ankle and wrapped it several times in rope before securing it to the bed post. He bound the right next, spreading her legs farther for easier access. With exact movements that spoke of his years of experience, Master Gannon tied her wrists together, then pulled hard so that she was stretched out seductively, her cheek resting against the mattress as he secured her hands to the headboard.

Gannon slapped her on the ass before he left. All the toys were now bound and ready for play…

"Having fun yet?" Mary whispered.

Brie smiled, purring, "Actually, yes. You know how I love the feel of rope."

Mary chuckled. "Yeah, you're a total freak about it."

"So when will the Doms come to play?"

"Not for another half-hour or so. Master Gannon

wants the toys eager for their attention."

"Shh," one of the other subs cautioned.

Brie understood that this forced waiting period had multiple purposes. It encouraged each submissive to reflect on what was about to happen. It also helped to put them in the right frame of mind—as objects of pleasure, they were there to meet the Doms' needs. A toy's satisfaction and enjoyment were based solely in fulfilling those needs.

For Brie, however, it went far deeper than that.

This extra time allowed her to ponder how similar this was to her first night at the Submissive Training Center. To be under the power of a stranger was both unsettling and exhilarating.

Just as she had when she'd scened with Ms. Clark for the first time, Brie decided to imagine that each Dom who came to her that night was *her* Dominant, the one she'd willingly given her body and heart to. It made the connection meaningful to her, and would translate into a more pleasing exchange for them both.

From the other side of the beds, she heard a distinctive and familiar sound. The loud buzzing of a Magic Wand cut through the heavy silence in the room. Soon the moans of the first toy followed, announcing her orgasm.

Brie whispered to Mary, "What's going on?"

"Master Gannon wants the toys eager and wet."

Brie listened to the erotic sounds as each sub orgasmed under the power of that wicked instrument, knowing her turn was coming. She stiffened when she felt a hand on her thigh and then the touch of the wand, but there was no escaping its merciless vibration or the immediate fire it incited.

"Don't fight it," she was told.

Brie willingly obeyed, and the juicy sound of her wet excitement joined the energetic hum. She cried out when her pussy pulsed in heated release.

Nothing was said, but the Magic Wand stopped buzzing and pulled away. With her wet clit still throbbing, she listened to the sounds of people making final adjustments to the playroom equipment before the room fell silent.

Brie's loins contracted in fearful pleasure—soon the Dominants would be coming to play...

Mary had explained that the Dominants warmed up using the toys before the other submissives were allowed to join the event. Releasing their needs beforehand allowed the Doms to concentrate fully on their BDSM scenes rather than their sexual urges. If at any point during the event they felt the need to release again, they could return to one of the many waiting toys.

Mary admitted to Brie that she preferred to be a playmate rather than a toy, but had bitten the bullet just for her. It was little things like that which let her know Mary considered her a friend, no matter how much the woman denied it. Blonde Nemesis was not one to normally sacrifice for another.

Brie whispered, "Thanks for doing this with me."

"Hey, I wasn't about to deny you your one chance to live."

The sound of low, male voices and the sultry pitch of females filled the massive room as the Dominants entered the dungeon.

"Welcome to the Dungeon, my fellow Dominants," Master Gannon announced. "The Toy Station has been primed and is ready for use."

Brie felt a moment of panic, but Tono's gentle command resonated in her head and she slowed her breathing, calming herself. This was not an experience Sir wanted her to 'survive', this was something he expected her to enjoy and learn from.

"Well, well, are you hard for me, toy?" a Domme asked down the line. Brie heard the sound of slapping and the primal grunts of the sub in response. Her pussy pulsated in reaction to their erotic exchange.

Soon the sounds of grunts, creaking beds, and moans filled the dungeon. Yet both Mary and Brie remained untouched.

How humiliating would it be *not* to be chosen the entire event?

"I knew you would be waiting for me," a gravelly voice stated, dripping with masculine arrogance. It sent chills down Brie's spine. She breathed an audible sigh of relief when it was Mary, not she, whom Razor chose to play with.

Mary cried out unexpectedly.

"That's right. I am going to treat you like the slut you are."

Mary purred, before the sound of slapping skin and whimpers ensued. Brie lay there helplessly, listening to the Doms and Dommes enjoying the other toys. After a while, she resigned herself to the fact she was only going to be a forgotten observer.

Then the steady footsteps of a man in boots approached her bed, the smell of his unfamiliar, musky cologne surrounding her. Brie slowed down her breathing even more as she willing gave in to her role.

This is it…

She experienced a moment of disappointment and partial relief when he moved away. However, it wasn't long before the footsteps returned. She gasped when she felt the touch of a wooden paddle on her ass. He caressed her skin with it for several moments before he lifted the instrument. She bit her lip, waiting for the impact.

It came down hard, harder than she was used to, and she yelped in surprise from the sting of it. Several of the Doms beside her chuckled, causing Brie to clam up. The last thing she wanted was to make a poor impression.

The paddle came down again and she grunted, her ass burning from the contact. He continued to rain down a volley of swats. Brie whimpered quietly, willing it to end. When he finally stopped, he resumed caressing her ass with the paddle.

Brie let out a sigh, appreciative that the pain quickly dissipated into a warm ache. She could tell the man playing with her was a skilled Dom, and it helped to ease her fear when he started up again.

Tears soaked her blindfold, but she did not cry out. When he stopped the second time, she heard him place the paddle on the table beside her. As she lay there trembling, she heard the distinctive sound of pants being unzipped, which was soon followed by the slight crinkle as he tore the wrapper off a condom.

There was a moment of panic—and Brie almost called her safeword.

However, she couldn't deny that she was excited by the slippery sound of lubricant being slathered over a hard cock, her body pulsed with the need to be filled by it, so she said nothing as the Dom moved to the edge of the bed.

He pressed his shaft against the valley between her ass cheeks and Brie let out a soft whimper of surrender. When his hands glided over her skin, she felt an unexpected jolt of electricity.

"Sir?" she whispered.

He leaned down and growled into her ear. "No, I am your Khan, and you are my final virgin for the evening."

She shivered in pleasure as it dawned on her that this was his version of her fantasy: all the subs tied up, waiting to be taken just like the virgins in her story, the giving of herself to a stranger, the King—or in her case, her Khan.

Brie kept in character, receiving his caresses as if they were from her sovereign Lord, but truly there was no need for her to roleplay. His unexpected visit had her on an emotional high that she couldn't contain.

She knew he would be rough with her, because that had been her fantasy, and oh, how she *wanted* to be used by her King. This environment was the perfect set up for it.

"I desire to claim this pink little ass," he said, chuckling arrogantly as he slapped her buttocks. She was taken by surprise when he stuffed her mouth with a cloth. "But I don't want to hear your screams when I fuck your virginal hole."

He positioned his cock against her anus and plunged in without any warning, letting her know he was taking his role as Khan very seriously. She groaned into the cloth, forcing her body to accept the full length of him. He pushed her face down into the mattress as he thrust deeper and harder, grunting with effort.

Brie's ass was on fire. He fisted her hair and pulled her head back, challenging her body with his rough handling. She panted into the dry cloth, surprised by the force and fierceness of his claiming but reveling in the first flutterings of subspace. She moaned when he let go of her hair, clutching her waist to thrust at a new, more demanding angle.

Reality blurred as she became focused solely on his royal shaft. Every part of her was concentrated on the fiery buildup he was creating as he pounded her without mercy.

So this is what it feels like to be possessed by a king...

Just when she felt she was on the precipice, he pulled out. Brie whimpered, suddenly feeling lost and desperate. He removed the cloth from her mouth and growled into her ear, "But I do want to hear your screams when I fill you with my seed, girl."

She heard the sound of a condom being removed and was soon rewarded with the head of his naked shaft against her aching pussy. He pressed his thumb into her sore ass, asserting his authority over her body.

Changing tactics, he took her pussy slowly, making her feel every inch of him as he buried his rigid shaft in her. "I will ruin you for other men."

With that pronouncement, he began stroking her pussy with long, slow thrusts as he pressed his thumb deeper. She moaned loudly, wanting him to hear the depth of her desire. The initial pulsing of an impending orgasm began deep within her core, growing in power as he coaxed it with his skillful manipulation.

She whimpered again, afraid the intensity of it might prove too much, but she was helpless to prevent what was coming. Her Khan was in control...

"Feel the heat of my pleasure, girl," he roared, his thrusts coming hard and fast as he released his seed deep within her. It started a chain reaction as her nipples contracted into hard buds while her pussy clenched his pulsing shaft, milking it with her own orgasmic release.

Brie screamed as she lost herself to the power of it, almost losing touch with reality as she came with violent force. She couldn't stop shaking afterwards, her body still reverberating from the fierceness of the release. "Oh, my God...oh, my God..." she whispered repeatedly, overwhelmed by the intense experience.

Sir began untying her, rubbing his hands over the marks on her skin caused by the tight binding. She smiled lazily when she was finally freed from the last of the rope, her hair damp from tears and well-earned sweat.

"I love you, babygirl," Sir whispered as he lay on the bed and positioned her rag-doll body on top of him. He untied her blindfold, then began stroking her hair, sending delightful shivers down her spine.

"I'm floating..." she murmured, nestling against him as she closed her eyes.

She heard Faelan beside them, taking his turn with Mary. It was an erotic exchange, animalistic and primal, but through it all she sensed the undercurrent of love between them.

As Brie lay in Sir's arms, she felt as if she were flying on a cloud of contented ecstasy, listening to the sounds of all the dungeon-play around her. The lashing of whips, the clanking of chains, and the cries of passion and pain—it felt like home to her.

Before Faelan left the Toy Station, he addressed Sir. "Glad you could make it, Sir Davis."

"This has been a remarkable experience, Wallace."

"You two can retire to our room, if you would like," Faelan offered.

Mary spoke up. "Wait, where am I—?"

Faelan put his fingers to her lips. "I've already arranged our evening, toy. Another outburst from you, and you'll be reported."

She looked up at him and smiled, then turned to Sir, nodding respectfully to him.

Sir acknowledged the gesture but did not speak to Mary. Instead he lifted Brie off him and commanded her to kneel. To her surprise, he left her alone there, not explaining his actions.

Brie knelt beside the bed, her hands behind her back, her chest out and her head bowed, but she couldn't keep from smiling. Sir was here...

He returned minutes later with a sponge, towel and bowl of soapy water. She purred as the warm sponge glided across her skin.

"Our rambunctious play has left you a bit untidy."

The best kind of messy, Brie thought as she spread her legs wider and felt his essence trickle down her leg.

He smiled to himself as he meticulously washed every inch of her skin. Once he was done, he gently toweled her off. The act was intimate and tender, his own brand of aftercare following his rough use of her.

Sir handed over the sponge, bowl and towel. "Return the items and meet me downstairs."

Brie walked through the dungeon, naked and proud. Maybe the Doms only saw her as a ghost, but she knew who she was. She was Sir's collared submissive.

Her heart swelled with pride when she walked into Mary's bedroom and found Sir waiting for her with open arms. "Come to me, Brie."

She glided to him, grateful to be in his embrace.

"Did you enjoy your fantasy?"

"It was a perfect interpretation, Sir. I am in awe."

"You didn't suspect I was coming today?" he asked, as he wrapped his arms around her. She curled up against him, laying her head on his chest.

"No, not for a second."

"I was actually concerned you might call your safeword before I had a chance to play with you."

"I came close, Sir," she admitted with a giggle. Brie traced the muscles of his chest with her finger, loving the feel of his rough hair. "You are a very devious Master."

His smirk let her know he had something else up his sleeve.

She propped herself on his chest. "Okay, what aren't you telling me, Sir?" she demanded playfully.

"I have an unexpected trip to make."

"Can I join you?"

"I'm unsure you'll want to. Unless, of course, you fancy the taste of vodka."

"Russia, Sir?" Brie squealed in delight.

Sir chuckled. "My Moscow client has encountered a problem I must address. I also was told that a certain Ruski holds out hope of being part of your documentary, so a Russia trip may actually prove useful to you."

"That would be incredible!" she said, bubbling over with excitement. "I was hoping to film the dynamic between a sadist and masochist."

"Well, now you'll have that opportunity." He pulled her against him and inhaled. "I miss the smell of you when we're apart. I find the fragrance of Brie intoxicating." She giggled as he began sniffing her body, but those giggles quickly quieted when he moved between her legs and his tongue made contact with her sensitive clit. "I think this Brie needs to be consumed."

"Oh, Sir…"

Broken

Faelan sought Brie out the next afternoon. "Have you seen Mary?"

"She left after lunch. Didn't tell me where she was headed, though." Brie could feel his anxiety, but was unsure of the cause. "What? Is something wrong?"

"I suspect she's with Razor right now."

Brie had noticed Mary's unnatural attraction to the fierce Dom. It wasn't a sexual attraction, but something darker and more insidious. "I'll help you look for her."

After searching the main building and barn, they headed out towards the woods. When they heard Mary's screams, they sprinted in the direction of her cries and found her bound to a tree. Razor was slapping her face with such force that it was already leaving bruises.

"Stop!" Faelan demanded.

Razor looked at him with surprise, but stepped away, growling, "I'm only giving the lady what she wants."

"I understand. It's not you I have an issue with." Faelan said, ignoring Razor as he approached Mary. She was slow to respond, the endorphins having kicked in from their violent play, but she turned her head to face Faelan with a look of defiance.

"Why are you going down this path again?" he asked, sympathy coloring the anger in his voice.

Mary frowned, and replied with disdain, "Fuck you, Faelan."

"I won't do this again. You were free of your father's influence; why are you choosing to return by playing out your past now?"

Her lip trembled for a moment, but she shook it off and lashed out angrily. "You don't know what I want or need!"

Faelan began untying her from the tree. "You are like an addict, incapable of staying away from the one thing that will destroy you."

"Don't be so overdramatic, asshole. And stop treating me like a child."

As soon as she was free, he pushed her up against the tree. "I told you *never* to do this again and yet you defy me?"

Her answer dripped with insolence. "Yes."

"I can't—I won't do this anymore with you." He let go of her. "You have a choice, Mary. You can stop pursuing your past or drown in it."

She shot daggers of hate in her gaze as she raised her chin defiantly to him.

"Fine." Faelan backed away from her slowly, with a look of resignation and overwhelming sadness in his eyes. "Goodbye, Mary."

The words sounded so final that it frightened Brie. "Don't do this. You're both upset. Why don't you discuss this when you've had time to calm down?"

Faelan looked at Brie, his blue eyes communicating his resolve. "She made her choice the moment she sought Razor out for this scene. There is nothing more to say."

He walked away, not looking back when Mary called out to him. When he didn't respond, she turned to Brie and rolled her eyes. "Such a fucking drama queen…"

"Go after him," Brie implored.

"He'll be back."

"No, Mary. He won't."

Mary gave an insolent laugh. "Oh, he'll be back. The poor boy can't get enough of me."

Razor chuckled as he grabbed her roughly by the throat. "Then let's finish what we started, slut." He spat in her face as he slammed her against the tree.

"Hit me again."

Brie turned away. It was heartbreaking that Mary was encouraging her own destruction. She watched in desperation as Faelan disappeared into the woods.

"Damn it, Mary. If you don't go after him right now, you'll lose him."

When Blonde Nemesis acted as though she hadn't heard, Brie started after Faelan, shouting behind her, "You're a fucking fool, Mary!"

"And you're a stupid bitch!"

Brie could not catch up, and lost Faelan long before she made it back to the lodge. She saw Sir talking to a group of Dominants and ran to him, panting for breath.

Sir excused himself and led Brie to a private spot, obviously concerned for her. "What's wrong, Brie?"

"Todd's run off. Mary defied him and he says he's done with her." Tears started to fall when she confessed, "She needs him, Sir."

Instead of becoming concerned, Sir pulled Brie into his arms. "I was afraid it would end this way."

She looked up at him in disbelief. "Why would you say that?"

"Wallace spoke to me about Mary's attraction to the newest Dom. Unfortunately, the man bears a striking resemblance to her father."

Brie suddenly felt nauseated. "Oh no…"

"Wallace is doing the right thing. Her defiance of his direct command cemented her fate."

"But they love each other," she insisted.

"Wallace has done what he can to ensure her well-being. Now he must concentrate on himself."

Brie felt a prickling on the back of her neck. "Sir, is there something wrong with Todd?"

The seriousness of Sir's expression confirmed her fears. "It's not for me to say. If Wallace wanted you to know, he would have shared it with you."

Brie's heart beat wildly, a feeling of panic setting in. "He can't leave Mary now. She has no idea, Sir. I'm sure of it."

"He didn't want to burden her, and ultimately it *is* his choice."

"But she would never let him go if she knew. It's not fair to her. I have to tell him!"

"I don't believe it would do any good."

The desperation she felt was overwhelming, and she begged, "Please, Sir."

He took pity on her, and told Brie, "Wallace went downstairs to pack. You may speak to him if he is still there."

She raced into the lodge and burst through the door to see Faelan closing his suitcase.

"There's nothing to be said, Brie," he barked.

"Whatever is wrong with you, Mary deserves to know."

His eyes narrowed. "What are you talking about?"

"I suspected something was wrong, and Sir just confirmed it but wouldn't tell me what."

He chuckled angrily. "Leave it to *you* to notice, when Mary didn't."

"She would never let you go if she knew, Todd."

"It makes no difference and wouldn't have changed what happened today."

"Trust me, if Mary knew—"

"This is something I have to face alone. She doesn't need to know and neither do you." He looked at Brie sternly. "I don't want Mary to know anything about it."

"But—"

"Do not defy me in this."

His tone took her certainty down a notch or two. Faelan was right. This was his life, his decision. It wasn't her place to intervene. "Fine, Todd. I won't."

"At this moment, Mary is basking in the belief that she has one-upped me, but once she realizes what she's done, she's going to fall hard." He looked at Brie with compassion. "If she reaches out to you, promise me you'll support her."

"But I'm so pissed with her now!"

"Feel free to hit her between the eyes with how you feel, the same way she would you, but be there for her nonetheless. I'm afraid she has chosen a path she won't recover from."

The look of loss on Faelan's face undid Brie. She walked over to him and placed her hand over his heart. "I'm sorry."

He looked at her with ocean-blue eyes haunted by deep sorrow. "I don't understand why I was spared on the day of the crash and not the boy I hit, because nothing I've done since has amounted to anything."

"No, that's not true," Brie protested. "I'm grateful to know you, and Mary is a better person because of you. Don't doubt that—never doubt that."

He shrugged. "Just be there for her, Brie. You're the only real friend she has."

"Of course. Can I at least ask where you're headed?"

He smiled sadly, shaking his head. "No, that's just between me and the powers above." He slung his duffle bag over his shoulder and grabbed the suitcase. "See you, blossom."

Tears blurred her vision as she watched him go, the lump in her throat making it impossible to speak.

But in her head she was crying, *Don't leave!*

Skeletons

Mary avoided Brie like the plague the last few days of her stay, choosing to bunk with another couple in a room at the other end of the lodge. Whenever an accidental meeting occurred, she treated Brie as if she didn't exist, although she acknowledged Sir.

"You are being very patient with her," Sir complimented Brie.

"I understand Mary. Despite her bravado, she knows she messed up—and bad. She just isn't ready to admit it yet, especially to me."

On the last day, however, Mary sought her out while Brie was taking in the mountain scenery from the bridge; the same bridge where Faelan had met with Brie on the first day.

"So you're headed back into the vanilla world, huh?"

"Yes, but I'm going to miss this place."

"Yeah, you're going to wish you could come back here, I bet."

Brie smiled, glad they were talking. "I'm sure I will."

Mary shifted uncomfortably on her feet. It took her

several minutes before she built up enough courage to say, "If you see Faelan, tell him I'm sorry."

"I will." Brie didn't have the heart to tell Mary that she had no way to pass on the message.

Mary looked broken when she confessed, "I don't think he's coming back."

Brie felt tears prick her eyes. "No, I don't think he will."

Mary glanced around and stated, "Here I am, living the dream, and it doesn't mean a damn thing without him."

"Brie," Sir said, walking up to them, "Gannon wants to speak to us before we leave."

"Certainly, Sir." She reached out to hug Mary and clasped her hand instead when the girl tried to pull away. "Look, I'm here for you. You can call if you need to talk, even though you'll have to head into Whitefish to do it."

Mary rolled her eyes. "Whatever."

Brie took the arm Sir offered and they headed towards Gannon's office. Mary called out to her, "You'd better accept the charges if I call, Stinky Cheese."

Brie turned around and laughed. "I make no promises, Mary Quite Contrary."

Master Gannon had an unexpected surprise for them when they reached his office. Brie had assumed he wanted to go over last-minute issues concerning the footage she'd shot. Instead, he handed Sir a large envelope. "It just arrived."

Sir took it from him and looked at the address of the sender. He glanced at Brie. "It's from my lawyer."

Brie held her breath, afraid she already knew what it

said. Sir tore open the envelope and read through the first letter with a questioning look. He shook his head and handed it to her while he read the second.

She looked it over with a growing sense of dread.

```
Dear Mr. Davis,

I didn't want to bring this issue to
your attention until I was certain it
was a legitimate concern. I received
this letter a week ago and requested
she submit a genetic test to verify her
claim. Normally, that is enough to
deter scam artists, but she has agreed
to the test.

    I await further instructions at your
earliest convenience.

Harold Thompson, Attorney at Law
```

Brie looked up and saw Sir with an expression of disbelief on his face. He read the letter again before handing it to her. Brie didn't want to take it, based on the look he gave her. She was sure it could only mean one thing—he was a father.

Brie noted that the woman's penmanship was as exquisite as Sir's.

Dear Thane Davis,

It is with a racing heart that I pen this letter to you. I have lived my life believing I was an only child. My mother, Ruth Elizabeth Meyers, never spoke of you, never once mentioned her life before my father, Jake Robert Meyers.

I can hardly think straight, and apologize if this letter makes no sense. I only just learned that my mother lies dying in a hospital in China. Even worse, I have been told that you may be seeking to end her life.

I beg you to spare her. Whatever your relationship was with my mother, you should know that she has always been good to me. I love her with all my heart, and cannot bear to lose her.

I hope you will agree to meet with me. Hopefully, we can come to a mutual decision concerning her future care and unravel the secrets she's kept hidden from us both.

I have no idea why she kept her past from me but, now that I know you exist, I feel desperate to meet you.

With earnest sincerity,
Lilly Meyers

Brie was stunned, and handed the letter back to him listlessly. He took it and read through it a third time.

Sir has a sister…

Why did that fill her with such foreboding?

Sir kept his cool, shaking Master Gannon's hand. "Thank you, Gannon. We have both enjoyed our stay here. You've created an environment for true community and sexual freedom that I didn't think possible. I'm impressed."

"I believe it should be the norm, not the exception." Master Gannon stated. He turned to Brie and shook her hand. "I hope the exposure you bring to my vision will incite change."

"That is my hope as well, Gannon. I will do my very best."

"I expect no less."

When they left Master Gannon's office, Rajah was there to meet them. Brie looked down when she felt the black cat rub against her leg. She smiled and picked him up, scratching under his chin.

Rajah looked at her strangely.

"What's wrong?" she asked, squeezing the cat against her.

"Shadow doesn't come to anyone but Master Gannon."

Brie smiled as she continued to pet the cat. "Really? He's been my friend during the entire stay here."

Rajah raised his eyebrow. "Master Gannon will find that fascinating."

Brie tried to hand the cat to him, but Shadow jumped out of her arms and ran out of the door. She giggled and shrugged. "Cats…"

"Pussies continue to remain a mystery to me," Rajah replied with a poker face as he handed Brie her car keys and cell phone. He then addressed Sir. "I've put your luggage in the trunk as well, Sir Davis. You are free to leave."

Brie asked Sir, "Didn't you drive here?"

"No, my dear. I flew in by private plane and landed a few miles from the commune on the morning of the dungeon event. Gannon picked me up personally. You had no idea that I was speaking to you from inside the main building when you called from Gannon's office?"

Brie shook her head. "A man of many surprises."

He looked at the papers in his hand. "Some I'm not even aware of."

Once they were on the road and could talk privately, Brie asked, "Do you think there's a possibility the woman's telling the truth, Sir?"

He glanced at her, shaking his head. "Frankly, I was expecting a false paternity suit."

Brie didn't want to admit she'd immediately assumed he was a father. She felt guilty now, knowing it showed a lack of trust in his honor that Sir did not deserve.

He continued, "Having a sibling was never a consideration. I will not give it another thought unless the test results confirm her claim."

"Do you want to head back to LA, then?"

"Brie, there is no need to concern ourselves about this when all we have to go on is a simple letter. The world is full of unscrupulous people. No, we move forward with our lives as if nothing has happened."

"As you wish."

"I've been looking forward to seeing Durov again, and we have yet to make use of the birthday present he gave you," he said, taking her hand and putting it to his lips. "Which is long overdue, babygirl."

The Parents

Once they were in the air, Sir explained that he had a short detour planned for them. Brie was elated, thinking that not only was she getting a trip to Russia, but an additional surprise as well. Those happy feelings died when she started noticing the familiar landscape of Nebraska outside the airplane window.

"We're visiting my parents, aren't we?"

"Yes. Although we've spoken to them about the wedding date, your parents deserve to be part of the planning process. It's tradition, is it not?"

"Yes, but normally the bride knows *where* she's getting married."

Sir smiled charmingly. "Nothing about us is normal, babygirl."

"You aren't planning on telling them the location, are you?"

"Naturally."

"How is that fair?"

"This is not about being fair, Brie." He kissed her hand, grinning with a mischievous glint in his eye. "It's about planning an event that will enchant you."

"But I hate surprises."

"No, you don't," he corrected. "You hate having to wait."

A young boy peeked his head over the seat and stared at them.

Sir continued, "As I am a responsible Ma—" he looked at the child and amended his next word, "...man, I must provide you with lessons in patience."

"You try my patience, Sir," Brie replied, pouting.

He chuckled, nodding to the child who was staring at him so intently. "I must continually provide her with lessons because she's such a stubborn pupil."

The little boy's eyes grew wide at actually being acknowledged by Sir, and he quickly popped back down in his seat.

Brie grinned. It was heartwarming to see her Master interacting with a child.

Sir turned to Brie. "I firmly believe in the saying 'Spare the rod, spoil the child'." He kissed her on the lips and whispered huskily, "But it may be because I enjoy using my rod on you—repeatedly." Her stomach fluttered at his words.

She could only giggle when the little boy popped his head up again.

As they pulled up to her parents' home, Brie's stomach trembled for a different reason. "This should be a good visit, right?"

Sir held out his hand and helped Brie out of the car. "I'm unsure. Although your parents have accepted your choice of husband, I don't get the impression they're happy about it."

"Then, Sir, may I ask why you keep putting us through this?"

"I believe in showing people the respect owed them. Your parents did a fine job raising you and deserve to be a part of your life now. Just because they dislike me, should not preclude them from seeing you."

"But it hurts my heart when they're rude to you," she said, stepping reluctantly onto the porch.

"I'm quite capable of handling their displeasure, Brie. Don't let that be a concern. I trust the bonds we create now will eventually mend the rift between us."

Brie shook her head. "If my parents understood how wonderful you truly are, they would greet you with open arms and a bottle of champagne."

"Possibly," he said with a smirk as he rang the doorbell.

Brie's mother opened the door, smiling shyly at Sir. "Please, won't you come in?"

"Mom!" Brie cried, stepping inside to hug her.

She felt her mother's muscles relax in her arms as they embraced. After a couple of seconds, Brie relaxed as well—it felt good to be in her mother's arms again.

"It seems like ages since we've seen you, Brie," her mother complained lightly as she took Sir's jacket and Brie's purse. She nodded them towards the living room. "Please make yourselves comfortable."

Brie was embarrassed to see her father sitting in his chair, purposely choosing not to stand up to greet them. Her father's slight did not deter Sir. He walked straight over to the man and held out his hand. "Pleasure to see you again, Mr. Bennett."

Her father could not take Sir's intense stare and stood up, shaking his hand. "Forgive me if I seem less than excited to see you, Mr. Davis. My experience has been that your visits only herald bad news."

"Wait," Brie piped up. "The first time I came I introduced my new boyfriend to you, and the second time I told you about my documentary."

"Exactly. If you look at it from our perspective, neither was exactly good news—now, was it?"

Brie stepped back, deeply hurt by his answer, but her mother put her arms around Brie's shoulders. "Your father is mistaken. Meeting Thane was certainly a shock, but we are both pleased to see you so happy. As for the documentary, although it was followed by much unpleasantness, we are proud of your accomplishment."

Her father looked as if he was about to say something, but wisely changed his mind and sat back down. "Pardon me if I'm not anxious to hear what you have to tell us today."

Sir sat down and pulled Brie next to him when she sat on the couch. "As you know, we have a date set for the wedding and would like you to be a part of the planning process."

Brie's mother's eyes lit up. "Really?"

Sir's smile was engaging and genuine when he told her, "Yes, Mrs. Bennett—it would mean a lot to Brie and

I."

"Oh, you can call me Mom if you want to," her mother replied, blushing profusely.

Brie's father cleared his throat. "I do not think I could ever get used to a man nearly my age calling me Father."

Sir turned to him. "And yet you will." He took Brie's hand in his. "Family is important to us."

"Look, I know why you're here, Mr. Davis. You act all formal and superior, but the reality is that you came to ask us to pay for this wedding."

Sir shook his head, amusement on his face. "As you so eloquently pointed out, I am *old* enough to finance our wedding. No, your involvement would be purely your choice—with Brie's approval, of course. In the end, it is the bride we all seek to please."

Brie felt heat rise to her cheeks. Hearing Sir refer to her as his bride was all kinds of romantic.

"Brianna, do you plan to come back here to marry?" her father asked.

"Actually, Dad, I have no idea where we're getting married."

Her father turned on Sir, his voice tainted with self-righteous venom. "Is this another example of you controlling my daughter, Mr. Davis?"

Sir patted Brie's hand gently. "No. I enjoy surprising Brie, and in this case it's strategic. While I devote my attention to the wedding, it gives Brie time to finish filming her documentary."

Now all her father's attention was riveted back on Brie, his tone stern. "What documentary, daughter?"

"Dad, I was asked to film a sequel."

"Not again!" he bellowed. "Didn't you put us through enough hell the first time? We've just barely recovered from the humiliation. What is this, Marcy?" he exclaimed, turning to Brie's mother. "Why must we continually be disgraced by our only child?"

Her mother wrung her hands nervously. "Another film, Brie?"

"I thought you would be happy for me, Mom. Although the first one met with some resistance, overall it was received positively by the film industry."

Her father frowned. "It was *not* a positive experience, young lady. Maybe for you, but certainly not for us." He turned savagely on Sir. "Why the hell are you letting her do this again? You *know* what happened last time."

"Mr. Bennett, this is your daughter's career, not mine. As her fiancé, I support her decision to do this second film and will help her complete the project in any way I can."

Her father was not pleased by Sir's reply and turned to Brie. "Brianna, time and time again you have proven how childish you are. It's as if you go out of your way to test us. Why? Aren't you too old to play the rebellious teenager?"

Brie's lip trembled as she fought to keep back the tears. She wanted to respond, longed to put her father in his place, but she sat there mute—as helpless as a baby.

"Brie," her mother said kindly, "Are you sure this is the best direction for your career? I know you once dreamed of making romantic comedies. If you do this second documentary, what chance have you got of being taken seriously?"

"Mom, I was a kid when I told you that. Things have changed since then—my dreams have taken a new direction. Trust me when I say that this film is important to me. I'm proud of my work and I believe in it so strongly that I'm willing to face your disappointment," she turned to her father, adding, "*and* unfair judgments."

"I can't believe we're being forced to go down this road again," he growled.

Sir squeezed Brie's hand. "Family is important to us, Mr. Bennett, and I trust it is important to you." Brie heard the raw emotion in his voice, and looked up at Sir in concern when he shared, "You know that I lost my father years ago. I can't tell you what I would give to have him in my life now, and yet here you are, throwing away your relationship with Brie as if it means nothing to you."

"I believe in tough love, Mr. Davis. You don't coddle people when they're making bad decisions."

"Then I have to ask, who do you see when you look at your daughter? I see an intelligent woman, full of compassion and grace, working hard in her career but also seeking to build a fulfilling life outside it. Isn't that good enough for you?"

"Damn it, man, I'm not the bad guy here!"

Sir's voice remained calm, despite the implied insult. "Although your daughter has chosen to pursue a path you don't agree with, it doesn't change the fact that she is still your daughter. Is your love and acceptance based solely on what you think she should be?"

Brie's father's angry laughter filled the room. "Oh,

that's rich coming from the man who controls my daughter's every move as her 'Master'."

"What you fail to understand is that I hold Brie in the highest regard. If she wanted to stop with the film and move in another direction, I would fully support her in that. Let me be perfectly clear, Mr. Bennett, Brie is in control of her life. I simply enjoy tweaking some of the details."

"And he's wonderful at that," Brie answered, wrapping her arms around him and kissing Sir on the cheek.

Brie knew the show of affection was difficult on her father, and wasn't surprised when he snapped, "I still maintain that her life would be *very* different if she hadn't met you."

Sir nodded. "I do not disagree. The question you must ask yourself is if that 'other life' you so desperately cling to is worth losing your daughter over."

"Brie *is* very happy, dear," her mother declared bravely, siding with Brie. "And they came to us to ask us to help with the wedding. Weren't you saying just last week how disappointed you were that we weren't being included?"

"No need to bring that up in front of these two," her father huffed in irritation.

Brie couldn't help but smile. Sir had been right. Her parents did want to be part of the wedding, despite her dad's bullheaded attitude.

"It would mean a lot to me," Brie confessed, putting her hand on Sir's knee. Then she corrected herself, "…to *us* if you would help plan the wedding." She turned to her father. "Please, Daddy."

For the first time that evening, her father's expression softened.

Her mother dabbed her eyes. "I can't believe my little girl is really getting married."

Brie stood up and walked over to her. "I would love it if you'd help me pick out the wedding dress, Mom." Her mother became a puddle of tears when Brie wrapped her arms around her.

When Brie turned and approached her father, he rose back to his feet. "Dad, having you walk me down the aisle means everything to me."

He held out his arms, squeezing her hard when she ran into them. "I'm your father—of course I'll walk you down the aisle." He kissed the top of her head. "That's my job, little girl."

Brie's mother joined them and they shared an impromptu group hug. "Your happiness is all that counts to your father and I."

Her father pulled away, furrowing his brow. "But that doesn't give you permission to become a Bridezilla."

Her mother laughed. "A what?"

"A Bridezilla. I've seen them on TV. It's disgusting."

Her mother shook her head, playing with a strand of Brie's hair. "Our little girl is no Bridezilla, Bill. I don't know why you even brought that up."

"Mr. and Mrs. Bennett," Sir interrupted, "I would like to fill you in on the specifics without Brie being present. Can we retire to the study?"

Brie refrained from whining when the three headed towards the study, but she was delighted when her mother looked back and announced, "Bill can fill me in later. I'll just spend time with Brie while you men talk."

"But Marcy…" her father implored.

She laughed, patting his arm. "You don't need to be afraid of your future son-in-law, honey. He isn't going to bite."

Brie wondered what Sir thought of being called 'son', but his expression didn't change as he followed her father into the room and shut the door. She trusted the conversation would be far more agreeable than the last one they'd had in that study.

"So, sweetie, tell me all about this second film…"

Brie spent the next half-hour nervously glancing at the door as she shared about Tokyo and Denver, the LA sessions and the Montana commune with her mother.

Her mom took it all in, shaking her head in disbelief. When Brie finished, she replied hesitantly, "It sounds fascinating, dear." Brie found the response cute coming from her mother.

Both women jumped when the study door finally opened.

Brie looked to Sir first, and was glad to see a pleasant expression on his face. "Then we're agreed. We'll have Mrs. Bennett fly down in a month to help Brie pick out a wedding dress."

"What's this?! I get to visit you in LA?" her mother asked with glee, then she immediately scolded Sir. "You really have to start calling me Mom."

Brie thought she saw a flush of color on Sir's cheeks when he answered, "Yes…Mom."

"That's more like it, dear," she said, giving him a maternal hug.

The bemused expression on Sir's face when he looked over her shoulder at Brie was freaking adorable.

Before they left for the airport, Sir handed her father a memory stick. "This is a piece Brie filmed that will not be included in the documentary. It involves a flogging scene with Marquis Gray. Your daughter not only filmed it, but was part of the scene itself. I hope you will consider watching so you can see the beauty of the exchange."

Her father hesitantly took it from him.

Sir continued, "Marquis Gray is an undisputed expert with the tool, but you'll see how exceptional your daughter is as well."

"He doesn't have sex with her, does he?"

"No, it's simply a flogging scene," Sir assured him.

Her father stared hard at the memory stick. "Mr. Gray did say it's therapeutic, that flogging 'thing' he does…"

"Therapeutic and breathtaking," Brie agreed.

Her father set it on the coffee table. "I'll consider watching it."

"Good." Sir held out his hand to him. "Until we meet again, Mr. Bennett. Before we leave, can you tell me if there's a carwash nearby?"

Brie was pleased that her father didn't hesitate to shake his hand this time as he answered, "Yes, a new one just opened two blocks south of here. You can't miss it."

"Perfect." Sir hugged Brie's mom, telling her, "And I'll see you in a month, Mom."

Brie's mother giggled like a young girl. "Oh, I can't wait!"

When they got into the car, Brie let out a long, happy sigh. "That went *way* better than I thought it would." She snuggled up to Sir before he started the car. "But only because you're brilliant, Sir."

"Brilliant may be overstating things a bit. The truth is your parents are easy to read. It's apparent that they love you, so my mission is to remind them of that whenever we steer off-course."

"Like I said, brilliant!" Brie insisted. He brushed his hand against her breast as she leaned over to playfully kiss him on the nose. The light touch caused tingles throughout her body.

Sir stared at her for a moment and then looked back at the house. "There's one more stop we need to make before we head off to the airport."

Sir pulled up to an automated carwash and Brie broke out in giggles as he painstakingly inserted his change, hitting the Deluxe Wash setting after he was done.

"Why are we washing a rental car, Sir?"

"Due to the lack of time before the flight *and* the lack of privacy on this particular plane, I have a challenge for you, téa."

She raised her eyebrow, smiling seductively at him. "Your wish is my command, Master."

Sir pulled the car onto the rails and set the vehicle in neutral. The machine gently guided the car along without the need of assistance.

He took his hands off the wheel and adjusted the seat back. Then he slowly unbuttoned his pants. The tingling she'd felt earlier traveled lower as she watched him free his cock from his boxers.

"Do you think you can bring me to completion before the car finishes the cycle?"

"It would be my honor." Brie got on her hands and knees, straddling the console to lean over Sir's rigid shaft. She looked up just as the soap bubbles covered the car in their rainbow colors. Giggling softly, she took his cock into her mouth, licking his frenulum teasingly before taking him deeper.

Sir groaned and pressed her head down farther onto his shaft. Knowing her time was limited and Sir's restraint was legendary, she began rapidly bobbing up and down, taking him deeper each time until her lips were nestled against his dark pubic hair.

She held herself there for several seconds, then pulled up to take a breath. Without missing a beat, her lips were back on his shaft. She started gagging as she tried to force it down too quickly.

"Slower, babygirl…I don't want you hurting that pretty throat."

She wiped away the tears that had formed from her efforts and tried again, being more careful to relax as she deep-throated him.

"Time's almost up," he warned gently.

She arched her back, thrusting her ass in the air. It was more enticing for Sir and gave her throat a new angle. In addition, she began moaning on his shaft, remembering what Mr. Gallant had taught her at the

Training Center.

It was enough to push Sir over the edge…

He groaned loudly as his hips rhythmically thrust his cock deep into her throat. After the last burst of come, he pushed her off of him. "Hurry, there are towel dryers."

She had no idea what he meant, but immediately flopped into her seat and swiped her mouth with her sleeve.

Sir didn't have time to zip up his pants, and casually pulled his white shirt over his open fly as two smiling attendants started hand-drying the car.

Brie looked at Sir in disbelief. "I barely met that challenge, Sir."

He hurried to adjust the seat back. "Neither of us was prepared for an audience at the end."

She waved gleefully at the men as they pulled away from the carwash, and watched in the side-view mirror as the two started ribbing each other. Brie suspected they knew exactly what had just transpired.

"I appreciate the opportunity to please you, Sir. You know I love it."

"I have another request."

"My pleasure, Sir."

"At the airport, after we have passed through security, I want you to take my belt and go to the restroom. Secure it under your dress, right about here." He touched the lower part of her abdomen just above her mound, making her heart race with the simple contact. "Make sure it's tight. I want you to feel the pressure of it the entire trip."

It was a wickedly cruel but sexy command. The last time she had flown to Russia, Sir had given her a lesson on belts in a private cabin. She would be reminded of that lesson the entire flight, without any hope of release.

"You know, I'm a tad surprised that Rytsar didn't insist on sending a jet for us, Sir."

"I left a message when I couldn't find a better flight, but he never called back. I have to assume he wasn't able to make arrangements on such short notice."

"But he does know we're coming?" Brie asked, remembering how Tono Nosaka had been surprised by their visit.

"He does, and I'm expecting his normal shenanigans when we get there. That could be the reason he hasn't returned my call—he's too busy planning his next prank. However, this time you and I are prepared. It's a waste of time on his part, but nothing can deter Durov once his mind is set."

Brie giggled, looking out the car window as they approached the Eppley Airfield. "I wonder what it will be this time…"

What does the wicked sadist have planned for Brie now—and can she handle it?

Find out in, *Trust Me.*

Buy the next in the series:

#1 (Teach Me)

#2 (Love Me)

#3 (Catch Me)

#4 (Try Me)

#5 (Protect Me)

#6 (Hold Me)

#7 (Surprise Me)

#8 (Trust Me)

#9 (Claim Me)

You can also buy the Audio Book!
Narrated by Pippa Jayne
Surprise Me #7

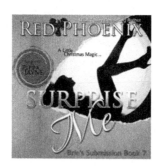

Brie's Submission series:

Teach Me #1
Love Me #2
Catch Me #3
Try Me #4
Protect Me #5
Hold Me #6
Surprise Me #7
Trust Me #8
Claim Me #9

You can find Red on:
Twitter: @redphoenix69
Website: RedPhoenix69.com
Facebook: RedPhoenix69

Keep up to date with the newest release of Brie by signing up for Red Phoenix's newsletter: redphoenix69.com/newsletter-signup

Red Phoenix is the author of:

Blissfully Undone
* Available in eBook and paperback
(Snowy Fun—Two people find themselves snowbound in a cabin where hidden love can flourish, taking one couple on a sensual journey into ménage à trois)

His Scottish Pet: Dom of the Ages
* Available in eBook and paperback
Audio Book: *His Scottish Pet: Dom of the Ages*
(Scottish Dom—A sexy Dom escapes to Scotland in the late 1400s. He encounters a waif who has the potential to free him from his tragic curse)

The Erotic Love Story of Amy and Troy
* Available in eBook and paperback
(Sexual Adventures—True love reigns, but fate continually throws Troy and Amy into the arms of others)

eBooks

Varick: The Reckoning

(Savory Vampire—A dark, sexy vampire story. The hero navigates the dangerous world he has been thrust into with lusty passion and a pure heart)

Keeper of the Wolf Clan (Keeper of Wolves, #1)

(Sexual Secrets—A virginal werewolf must act as the clan's mysterious Keeper)

The Keeper Finds Her Mate (Keeper of Wolves, #2)

(Second Chances—A young she-wolf must choose between old ties or new beginnings)

The Keeper Unites the Alphas (Keeper of Wolves, #3)

(Serious Consequences—The young she-wolf is captured by the rival clan)

Boxed Set: Keeper of Wolves Series (Books 1-3)

(Surprising Secrets—A secret so shocking it will rock Layla's world. The young she-wolf is put in a position of being able to save her werewolf clan or becoming the reason for its destruction)

Socrates Inspires Cherry to Blossom

(Satisfying Surrender—a mature and curvaceous woman becomes fascinated by an online Dom who has much to teach her)

By the Light of the Scottish Moon

(Saving Love—Two lost souls, the Moon, a werewolf and a death wish…)

In 9 Days

(Sweet Romance—A young girl falls in love with the new student, nicknamed 'the Freak')

---

9 Days and Counting

(Sacrificial Love—The sequel to In 9 Days delves into the emotional reunion of two longtime lovers)

And Then He Saved Me

(Saving Tenderness—When a young girl tries to kill herself, a man of great character intervenes with a love that heals)

Play With Me at Noon

(Seeking Fulfillment—A desperate wife lives out her fantasies by taking five different men in five days)

Connect with Red on Substance B

Substance B is a platform for independent authors to directly connect with their readers. Please visit Red's Substance B page where you can:

- Sign up for Red's newsletter
- Send a message to Red
- See all platforms where Red's books are sold

Visit Substance B today to learn more about your favorite independent authors.

CPSIA information can be obtained
at www.ICGtesting.com
Printed in the USA
LVOW04s1958211016

509751LV00008B/420/P